QUERENCIA

AUTUMN 2025

Querencia Press – Chicago Il

QUERENCIA PRESS
© Copyright 2025

All Rights Reserved

ISBN

978 1 963943 49 8

www.querenciapress.com

First Published in 2025

Querencia Press, LLC
Chicago IL

Printed & Bound in the United States of America

CONTENTS

POETRY

Pine / Pine

Pine needles bristle,
little emerald bayonets,
an army dripping

resin, oozing amber,
as if longing could
crystallize into hope.

I glut the ground
with clotted sap swelling
like malignant tumors,
like cones of eagerness.

Pine for being alive;
plant a seed; build a hive

of wanting; grow
to the height
of your appetite;

stretch skyward &
soothe your starvation.
Quench, choke, sputter—

bolster this conifer creature
to the soil which strangles it.

A pine does not die;
it is a great sylvan heaven,
it exhales, it sways, it conjures

this plague of desire,
this evergreen fever,
a lusty sickness that never
drops its leaves.

Ubiquitous, this photic pang
to split the bark & be seen.

I reach, reach; no one comes.

Only the wind, sucking,
gasping, never staying.

Pine for mercy.
Pine for forgiveness.

The pine sap hardens.
It was always too late.

—JORIE LOGAN (she/her)

IT'S ONLY THAT MY WIFE PORTIA SWALLOWED FIRE.

I am dependent on all the ways
by which famous literature's women
have killed themselves.
Oh, I'm so sorry, it's just
that after the neighbors
cut out my tongue and severed
my hands, I came into
possession of a dagger and finagled
its blade to my stomach
via stained, wrapped stumps.
Two weeks' notice
with upper management's
lecherous tongue still working
in my ear? A careful reiteration
of *please don't, thanks so much
for your understanding*
a strategic two meters
of institutional carpet
fixed between us?
Finagle your blade, girl.
Look, Ma—no hands.

—ABIGAIL KIRBY CONKLIN (she/her)

荒, beneath grass艹: the dead亡
and the river川. post-deluge,
gone were humans and beasts.
all ceased. weeds run
rampant. the uncultivated
新世, fruitless, yields
not a single grain. irrational is

荒芜: the abandoned
overgrown. 芒芴, the
trance beneath the grass.
unrecognizable, ungraspable.
an epiphany of as-if,
of awn and cress. the stupor
from semblance:

荒, remnants of fish.
Loose filaments, translucent,
opalescent and pliant. Implied
hollowness of the thorax,
weightless needles
birthed from the stripping
of decayables, bloodflesh
swallowed down, subsistence
is warmth that lingers
in our belly, 哀れな

荒よ, shrouding the food;
unhusked rice, its
dormant germ inchoate.
nascent civilization, people
polishing it with hands, traces
of domestication, persisting from
eight to thirteen centuries ago,
today's lucent teardrop shape,
plumule, 新世に―

荒れ: turmoils, chaotic
emotions, harsh words,
sloppy work. land unkempt,
jests ridiculous and arabesque,
indulgence, unfamiliar, flaws of
you and me, absurd
dramaturgy. the care
endures, indefinitely distant:

13

大荒. the old woman
on her deathbed, feverish,
in the desolate fields,
the scent of plum blossoms
is but a final, fleeting
dream. in this still-
denied anthropocene,
this crumbling boat—
to the new epoch

—TRACY CHENXI SHI (she/her)

Hyperbolizing as the Prince of Old Church Road

I am a boy of many gods, ten cents and I'll tell you how many

I've kissed

in the cherry-wood chapel across the lamprey river where the reverent shutters
the ache of his lips behind the confessional

A lover split seven ways, I serve not money, nor angels, nor the hieratic
assembly of ecclesia who have the gall to bind me to this ramshackle post

And still the collar, the bull-leather snatched around my ankle, demanding five
hundred hours of prostration before the magnified host

aloft the midnight altar

Trowel in hand, I forego the binding, carve out of myself a lambent ever of
moon bleached bone and precious blood

And I shall take the rising bridge of my own throat of my throat to open waters

—LORENA MARIA (they/them)

STRANGE FRUIT

I am walking my dog, Osito,
when a bullet finds its way into my chest.
I do not know who killed me.
Perhaps it was police
or a vigilante pretending to be police
or one of the neighbors
or the person who carved KKK into our sidewalk
or the man who waves two large Trump flags
or my friend who liked a post
that said Blue Lives Matter on Facebook.

After I am shot, my sternum cracks open,
my heart visible and beating, like the soft skin
beneath a hermit crab's shell. Cherry blossom petals
bloom from my chest.

My hand falls, hitting the concrete.
I try to hold onto Osito's leash. He licks my tears,
my ears, my hands, but I do not stir.
He steps in my blood on his way home,
his red footprints leading my family back to my body.

After I am gone, hornet's nests crash and crack.
Hornets fall like bullet casings hitting the ground.
The sky rips open like an angry gash, coughing up dozens
of white mourning doves with broken beaks.

Even when it rains, my blood remains. They replace the sidewalk
with fresh new slabs of cement, but my blood stain
seeps through. There are cherry blossom petals
strewn across the lawn,
but no tree.

—EVA LYNCH-COMER (she/her)

on your knees isn't low enough

how many Black girls got on their knees and erected this nation? just so you could tell them their daughters aren't good enough for you. i am not good enough for you. comment on how broad our shoulders are. question our femininity because we were built to carry the history of our people on our backs. who else would tell the truth? who else would tell our stories? who else would put fear in our children, in hopes they survive another day?

you take our husbands, sons, fathers, and brothers. lock them away and keep them for the safety of your people. this is not our land; you remind us of that with the forced segregation, renamed *gentrification*. no resources but our bodies and your dope. but our blood floods the concrete, as your troops march towards our unarmed men that are trying to get home to us. bullets spray, hands on the wheel, crying for mother and daughter.

you tempt us with idols like Michelle Obama and Serena Williams, start rumors of what's under their skirts. are they male or female? because you can't be strong and feminine. you can't echo resilience in heels. you can't be educated, articulate, be the best at anything and still be Black.

i remember the first time someone commented on my hips and thighs. i was young and not fully developed. they compared my ass to a kardashian. but the kardashians were not kardashian yet. kim was a woman on sites blocked at schools, smiling at the camera with spit running down her chin. i was being bullied. i didn't know this at the time. sexualized, and i blushed at the thought of being admired and sought after, desired.

some of us don't know the whole truth. are born to white mothers that don't teach us that our skin has a name. that people will look at us, scream out nigger, and make our skin crawl. with the footsteps of those that came before us. marching towards our mouths to put words in our throats that mimic the idea of a dream had, almost 60 years later.

you, the white people, that read this poem or hear it as it presses past my lips. will question the idea that we are no closer to freedom than we were 200 years ago. but there are more Black men incarcerated or under watch by the criminal justice system today than were enslaved in 1850. don't ask me how we fix this or how you can help. Black people built this country, taken from our homes, devoured by your hatred and greed.

always against our will.

i was born. not asked what skin color to choose. and even then, i am reminded that i am palatable. light enough to be unafraid to call bullshit. to give attitude to the cops that call me suspicious. to say the truth about what it feels like to fit the stereotype. that i will never know my father and people ask me if i blame him. how can i? when you're born to a dark-skinned man in modern day America, your first word is goodbye.

—ALEXIS RAYMOND (she/her)

Everybody knows that heat expands matter and cold compacts it. At the end of one day in middle school I suppose I preserved my heart in a jar like a sample to be dissected. But instead of prying fingers and the coldsteel kisses of a scalpel, it sat there in its icebox. It sat there hidden like a scar behind a sleeve. Over time, the heart hardened like a lover. Irony. Irony. Icebox became a

deathbox became a grave. I check on it, peeking timidly behind the freezer door. The discomfort, like visiting a crime scene long after the police tape has fluttered away. I see the violence in that jar, all purple and red, the swirling blood of its smile. Heart used to be so soft it would bend and crease under the impressions of everyone's fingers, the weight of touch

changing its shape. Now the flesh is smooth. Like a baby's conscience. Now it is pristine, solid. Indifferent. I don't like my feelings, don't like to talk about them. But some days, some days I want that heart back in me, want the courage taken from me to anoint my head and drip down my cheeks, dusting my lips like tears. I want the tears, some days, and someday I know all these feelings will rebel. I hear the cries of them, some nights, when I'm quiet and still, rigid like the heart in the glass.

Some nights I imagine this nightmare to lull me to sleep: I'm on the operating table. An emergency in my body and when they open me up, when they open me up all they hear is singing, shifting, screaming. My guts, my insides torn yet dancing. Shouting like they're on a rooftop and unafraid. Shouting because they have spent too long, afraid, inside me.

—NICO RICCIARDI (he/they)

—after Beth Dufford's the catalogue of daily fears

Bright grasses, yellow crescent, yellow stars. Any time under the light of a late summer harvest moon. You have me. We holler through indigo, hinder sleep, the hounds join us yelping to the stars. Rodents hide in, scamper under brush and into holes, tassel of tail winking in moonlight, a rattle shutters, the click of a twig. Stillness before venom and dinner, a rattle for friends. Music for children.

Use our love to discern liberty. Don't think it without sense. Or what we name it. For a country. For capital. War. Evil. The scythe of imagination, malevolent inventions. Only, hope. We need to be like this! To be listless and strain our bones. To speak with tenderness. To be content. Collar a mellow harvest moon. Sleep. Wake to a jackhammer, a sump pump, an idle motor, an ATV circling. The moment of our discontent. Again. It's comic. A Fed X flight circumnavigating the suburb. Cosmic nonsense or mother wisdom? Indeed, surrounded by beauty. We all love the children. Know best is best. Only, sheltered with love.

Awake, to a trumpet, to judgment, a desperate wail, peace, liberty. We have our ways. It's an experiment clouded with core puzzles. Corpuscles pressing to apprehend, a window through the sheer curtain that is "all mirror to the self." It is always like this. All creatures, splinter, ignite. Hark, a demand at a gate. Why the moral? Comply. No, light up without heat. Believe, like the self-same phases of the same moon constantly shifting in the same sky so it hangs yellow and wide and hands night the grin of a Cheshire cat. Its shade figures a seahorse frozen in the waves. How can I frame this emotional wisdom?

Love with a fever calling to be content, to speak with tenderness. For the most part I lasso your heart. A pink leather tassel glistens under a waning moon, one curved thorn of a smile peaks from a fig leaf. I am waxing heroic, but it's time to see the light in the sky. What, O what a feast, to fighter planes synced to canned laughter. What we let go of with shelter, love, sustenance, changing cacti into wax, sweet strings on a mellow guitar, the bright wink of a jam.

—Valyntina Grenier (she/her)

july cracked open

i get sick in the summer
when hot showers are too
uncomfortable to stomach
and drenched bedsheets do not confess
whether they arose from fever or
old heartbreak
i'm supposed to sleep better, this summer
regulated by tiny green pills and
a reliable night routine
but i watch the time paint
over layers of the sky
i swear it gets less dark every day
but i miss you, still
maybe even more
now that i can finally see the stars

—Kieran Fu (they/them)

21

no one cares
—after Diana Khoi Nguyen

cousin tells my mother
could say i'm
dysfunctional dys
violent wish i
didn't rhyme ma
wish i could stop
could stop writ
worrying wish i
wish i wish i wi
wishing is just
burn it up like a
emancipated unapo
know how to be
resting bitch life

your kids are successful i wish i
as autistic as dysfunctional
functional as violent violent
was nonverbal another poem
king saints kill themselves
writing about suicide wish i
ing about wish i could stop
could stop wish i could i
sh i wish i wish i wish i wish
gay prayer utada spilled
gay parade intoxicated
logetic hate that i don't
joyful resting bitch face

—DAVI SCHWEIZER (they/them)

THE HARVEST IS BARE

Memory is a fickle thing—a bushel of apples, the grunt of an old oak and
grasshoppers in the rain—trudging up the slime of a hill, I miss a step.
The harvest is bare—gobbled up by wildfires—my auburn landscape is
waylaid by an alien streak of red; a lone scarecrow folds over, the tadpoles
are motionless in the mud, and nocturnal visitors flounder in the night.
Yes, the harvest is bare and my bushel now empty.
There is nothing here for us.
The fields of my everything are claimed by another.
Hastening, I give way to these shadows that lengthen; and gracelessly, I
concede to the ghostly figures creeping out from under the sycamore tree.

—AGNEYA SINGH (he/him)

On this 9th Mother's Day After the Death of My Mother

My dad had records that ran
at 78 rpm. We thought we could

count out the reverb in our voices
as the chatter at dinner melded

our bodies with the plates
clinking together, my mom sick

of trying to blend in, bent into a depression
we couldn't sing, her muffled mutterings

an under-song of my dad's swing.
We learned to dance drying the dishes,

shifting places to fit between
the instant coffee & the cups—

a whole history of our lives together
still playing on the phonograph.

—CARLA SCHICK (they/them)

VESSELS

Noah ignores a drowning Eve;
after all, the animals need space.
Her tears are lost in the rushing deluge.
Maybe there's room on the Flying Dutchman?

Cruise ships sail like floating petri dishes
loaded high with endless shrimp.
The front half of the Titanic and Andrea Gail
hold on to each other for dear life.

Pi and his Tiger drift somewhere offshore
trying to get the story straight.
Old man Santiago finally lands a giant marlin.
Will he row it back to shore uneaten?

The crew of the Nautilus suffers from the bends.
A Yellow Submarine implodes.
The Mayflower gives one look and turns around,
only to crash bow-first into the Santa Maria.

—MAXWELL BAUMAN M.F.A. (he/ him)

Bomb Threats

in a building / where I perch
my body / our homes / banned
books / words that dissolve
with burnt / fingerprints / how can
there be love / without
touch / someone planted
a threat / in my throat /
I try to scream / to get out
of this trap / but the maze has me
running / an electric wire sparks
my toes / there is no rest / beneath
a scalding shower / they say I am not
a prisoner / but someone keeps me
pinned to the ground / I taste
earth / and seeds fall /
from my lips.

—CARLA SCHICK (they/them)

A couple throws a baby shower,
five hundred dollars' worth
of pink and blue balloons
bloated against a cloudless sky.

      At a traffic light,
      an old man clutches a sign,
      words wilting in the sun:
      Down on my luck.

Up the street,
a wedding is planned
on a budget big enough
to feed a village for an entire year.

      Somewhere in the Pacific,
      a whale feasts on its final plastic supper.

On the other side of the world,
olives fall from trees, unpicked.
A mother buries her child
in a grave dug with bare hands.
Empty pots sit cold on a stove.

      I dissolve the pill that stops
      the ceiling from crushing me.

Elsewhere, champagne froths
into gold-rimmed glasses.
A neighbor polishes the rims
of his lavish new convertible.

      The rich are getting hungrier,
      their souls: malnourished.

Tonight,
another billionaire
sharpens his teeth
on the bones of misfortune.

—ANA DEE (she/her)

Mamiwata
> —on "Mamiwata" artwork by Isabel M. Arche and Ramón M. Martín

i throw quarters in the ocean,
give beads of water to desert snakes.
write her name in my mirrors,
brush my hair with a fine-toothed comb,
rub mango juice on my skin before entering
the sea. dive underwater, close my eyes.
sing like a whale calling
to her love. low. legato.
water snakes wrap around
my arms, lift me to the surface.

mama sagrada
cuidame por siempre.

mamiwata watches me in the raindrops that gather
into puddles in the concrete, in the water
that swirls down my sink, in the steam
that fogs my window. i bathe with
rose petals and cinnamon, dip my head
between my legs, call yemaya. oshun. mami wata.
diosas del mar ayúdame. ven aquí, por favor,
porfa, por fin.

—EVA LYNCH-COMER (she/her)

I buy pre-made smoothie cups to make sure I am fed. The bottom of the blender fell out during the first one. You'll know the type of season I am speaking about. I keep the cats, you keep the desert. I got them in the mail the other day, and whatever part of me that is fell through the floorboards. There is a sedan with a golden arch license plate parked on our street this week, and I'll die before I look at it again. I went to a new Chinese medicine doctor, my tongue is back to putting up those red prickles. You went so quiet I couldn't get a word in. I write notes to insurance saying I sat with so and so for an hour today, they talked to me and I tried to talk back. I don't write that my throat closed so completely, I was still trying to reason with you. More empty heat. There is a young man in the cafe asking the woman next to him if he can plug in his charger behind her, asking what she is doing and where she is from. He wants her to look at him so badly he cannot shut up. I think how I can't remember my sexual orientation anymore. I ask the barista could I please go back in time and have syrup added to my latte? I thought I'd asked but I've learned better than to trust my memory. The coffee is gone, I leave with something missing. I learn that Carl Jung had everything to do with the twelve steps. He prescribed the numinous for chronic relapse, and voilà. Everything is coming together. I note that prayer is cognitive defusion. My fellowship is all online now and I mine for precision to make up for what's not in the air. The cats don't like the new house. It is too large and too dim, they are rowdier now. When I was four I had a birthday party. My parents bought a dalmatian piñata, and when the thing was strung up in the grapefruit tree, kids fighting with each other for the bat, I ran forward and yelled stop, don't hurt him. I stored ripening bananas in my dresser to save them from being eaten. My mother pilfered and discarded them while I was in school, when the ethylene reached the hallway. I think how thoroughly we cannibalized each other. The baby next door is not a baby anymore. She's got me on the walkie talkie, she wants to come and see the kitties.

—ELIZA FIXLER (she/her)

DE-POSSESSED

Who thrives in this special kind of ghostmealed winter? Where it snows a congealed chrome, crunching like an ice cone. Nothing sounds so loud. Is it a portal to memory, or a new realm forming as You choose to stay here, slipping out of an aura so crystalline with a hollow blueness.

The blistering sun dissecting You, stuffing your body with latency and inertia. The fiber gritting Your throat until you expel timefluid and static. Spitting it out forms the shape of You, but it isn't You.

The horizon is skipping again, isn't it? You're stuck shifting, pupils dilated with twilight, with sun. Lilac over wheat. Fragmentation as stillness. It's okay to need. I promise to be here, now, wherever this is, bound by wormpulsed sky in our block of vision.

—tommy wyatt blake (he/they)

31

people pleaser apologizes for people pleasing
—after L.I. Henley

this is an apology
to a long list of people
I don't know how I ended up on this side of things

but I am sorry, lovers
for not being enough
too much
never the right amount of enough
taking space I thought I had earned
after giving so much of it up to you

I'm sorry, friends or friends of friends
for expecting reciprocity of light and dark
a balance center justified

I'm sorry to my family
most importantly my mother
who wanted a pawn
but got a second daughter instead
now she doesn't even have that
for the daughter in me died
when I lost sight of the mother in her

You wanted control
I wanted love
that is all the same to you

This is your apology
a reprise of the same song and dance
I've memorized the lyrics and eight counts to

You expect it, perfect and rehearsed
Yet I changed the choreography

This is no longer an apology
but a call out to an unwanted muse.

—MAE FRASER (they/she/he)

CLUTCH

I am forever chasing it
        something that tastes like salt and want

my breath ghosts over her lips in a dream
        the way words come out in winter
        the way you only see the cold shape of them

I clutch hope like an anchor
hold it tight to my chest
lest I don't make it home
        before dark

—NICHOLAS OLAH (he/him)

BIRTHDAY CAKE, OR AN EARLY CONDOLENCE

The knife on the platter
is your portion of cake—
its ridges cut through the frosting
of life so gently,
so like your skin,
it cannot be called violence.

This is not contrast—
but distance,
measured and condensed
into your absence.

From the crowd
riding the waves
of the knife's grooves,
no one asks:

How did you gather
all your wounds
into your voice,
until even your silence
bore its own cuts?

And why—
with all the pressure
of those scars pressed together—
was no cry
ever freed?

—AREF MOALEMI (he/him)

paranoid helicopters/dead penguins

your kids are talking to pedophiles
on the website where you can be a penguin
decorate your igloo. you're invited because this party
                              isn't a party. you know where they are
                                        at all times.
                    longitude/latitude my
friends are being objectified on youtube.
people are obsessed with his vpl his
visible penis line his
verified pretty life.
the abuse form the abuse forms
the abuse doesn't feel real until.
someone comments on your video
shirtless underwear hype
with the sunglasses emoji
yeah that was fucking cool yeah.
that's what you ask for i could be a teenager.
your kids are talking to subs on bdsm forums yelling at them.
pay the ugly tax
pwincess valorie wants to go to
warped tour.

—DAVI SCHWEIZER (they/them)

Previously published by Trashlight Press

I STARE AT THE MIRROR AND SAY YOU

Believed you could be something other.
Could
Have
Been
Pulled towards the extraordinary on Helios'
Chariot & yet you missed its departure,
& the mourning dove's wailing.

Sustained by the fruits of your father's
Orchard, you suffer nothing and still know only
Flesh tremors & frigid plunges,

Think of your last elation. Of blueberry wine
& cherry liquor soaking your evening gown. How
old were you then? 17? 18? Waking required little ritual.

From your mother's great chasm, you were formed
& into that granite maw, you descend, mumbling, jaw loose,
With a pit rolling between your lips.

—LORENA MARIA (they/them)

GUILTY MONEY

Do you know
we really thought
we'd saved you?
The precarious house
of drugs and booze and blood
battering against
the age of being stupid
and the lost souls
at its helm.
How many times
did you say
and say again,
your utter disbelief
in how far we reached
to love you?
Departure cleaves.
The broken port
of self-importance, boats
cracked open in low tide.
The lobster fleet will rot through
before the turn of the season,
if this self-aggrandizement
keeps up. None of us
will have food to spare,
come Christmas. The act
is threaded through with rot.
I've seen this one, cut out
the white filigreed blooms
before turning
the remaining flesh into a pan
over medium heat.
The question is why
I keep insisting on its revival.
Mounting the increasingly
dog-eared sets, mouse-eaten
cables. I thought
it meant something
to keep loving someone.

Just as a furtive mouth
after the fifth drink
finds another, and the landing place
tastes like "I will stay
through nuclear fallout with you,
I swear on my fucking life."
My strange cruelty leaking free
like a comet tail,
better to let the world know
that someone was held
and someone let go. Where is the scroll
to unfurl? Here named
is everyone I
have ever loved.
Here is everyone I held.
Here is everyone
I kept loving
long after the lights
went down
and the electricity got cut
and I kept standing in the dark
half-believing I could make
light again.

—ABIGAIL KIRBY CONKLIN (she/her)

HOW TO BE A GIRL

To stand still is to risk atrophy,
beige walls, comfortable shoes.

I've practiced the dodge—a rolling stone,
stolen dialect sans dance card,
I've become an expert at moving.

I avoid elastic, accumulate fewer debts.
I measure happiness
in number of days
since my last midnight snack—

I don't ask my mother
the best place to meet men,
how to walk in heels,
why she doesn't call

> [*What's for dinner?*
> Means: *Are you eating all that?*
> Really means: *You disgust me.*
> *(You're disgusting)*]

nor for her blessing, don't wait for her to say
she's sorry, to hear she's proud.

> [*Girl:*
> *Don't buy yourself flowers.*
> *Don't laugh at your own jokes.]*

—CECILIA SAVALA (she/her)

the legality of a name

how legal is a name
when you cannot speak it through bloated tongue

I cannot pronounce the birthright
given to me by my mother
but maybe it's best to spite her
and quit stumbling over
something i never asked for.

—MAE FRASER (they/she/he)

I ghosted you two years ago, supposedly. I don't know. You had a weird request. I mean, you're not as bad as Thirsty Dad, who opened with "No way, you're 28. You look like you're 19. But if you are really 28, you look great!" And I guess I should be thankful it wasn't an old erect penis in my messages, but you know I don't delete the app, so I suppose it's my fault? It doesn't help that my username is send eggplant emoji. Anyway, you ask if you should stand up, and sure, there's a barrier and no cameras, but stand up? Why? You aren't nervous about getting caught. I think this is a misdemeanor or something? And yes, I have always wanted to fuck my teachers, sorry? My goody two-shoes, missionary Christian public speaking teacher had long legs and crackhead eyes, you know real big and doe-like. A philosophy professor who shouldn't have gotten the graduating teaching job at Temple U, he stuttered in every class. He seemed horrified that I was thankful for enjoying the class during the semester. Fuck, weird dude jerking off in the Staples, I'm still recording. I can't never read this out loud in front of people, scared to submit this, it's not about you, don't flatter yourself unless you want to flatter yourself and if you know what tribe you're on wink wink and which bunk bed you sleep in maybe maybe it's not your fault I promise I didn't zoom in on your balls, unless if you want that to be the focal shot? It's scary, a worker is coming, zip up your pants! I don't know what's wrong with me. Any aging twink giving me positive attention can set off an alarm for me to be flirtatious. It's odd, I should see a therapist, well, not the curious one who wanted to bottom, like maybe a woman therapist, and take it seriously this time.

—DAVI SCHWEIZER (they/them)

ONLY A COLD
Before They Called It Undetectable

I came before dark—always after.
Bleach stung the air like holy water.
I mouthed "anonymous," palms wet, voice dry.

Waited, guts knotted,
her stamps too sharp, her eyes too still,
like she knew.

A rosary pressed flat in my pocket—
God silent, but I carried Him anyway.
My shadow flinched at the door's click.

A cotton ball stuck to my arm,
too light to stop the shaking,
the blood already gone.

I didn't ask when results would come.
I stuffed the pamphlet deep,
maybe silence was better than knowing.

At home, the quiet pressed harder—
The Año Nuevo bottle sweated in the dark,
untouched, waiting for forgiveness.

I turned down my sister's bitten candy apple,
sweet and red as a wound.
My father's razor, warm with Old Spice.

I almost told him, not in words—
just dropped the towel, or didn't pull away—
but I couldn't risk what silence would change.

Around the guys, I kept my part:
legs wide on the bleachers,
voice never breaking.

Flat hands clapping backs.
My knees ached to close, but I held the pose.
Even my answers weren't mine.

Once, when he laughed,
I let myself join him—
for a moment, I wasn't a secret.

But when the others pressed, I stayed still.
His hand on my shoulder kept me awake.
I chewed back whatever wanted out.

Saw him change shirts—
pretended to tie my shoe,
memorized the slope of his back.

I slept alone, even when I didn't,
afraid I'd talk in my sleep,
that they'd hear what I loved.

I told myself it was only a cold.
But I knew—
his breath still warm on my back.

God doesn't ask these questions out loud.
I locked them in my chest,
praying He—and the results—couldn't read lips.

—JAIME RODRÍGUEZ (he/him)

About the Tattoo You Got to Remember Your Mother

I know it's a cardinal.
I know you kissed someone
ten years ago in pink pants.
I know the feel
of your tired bones
beneath the shifting
skin of your back. It was
always cardinals
your mother took note of
in the stacks of handwritten copy
you unearthed
in the weeks after.
She shouldn't have died
in that particular way.
You shouldn't have had cause
to discover her love
of the avian carousel
spiraling past her window
with each passing season.
Not yet, anyway.
I know there should've
meant to have been
more time.
You are owed.
The birds told me so.

—ABIGAIL KIRBY CONKLIN (she/her)

COTTAGE

We cluster in the kitchen in a pendulum of goodbyes,
skin pebbling in the cold—the promise of again
before the teetering accidents of time.

Missing you, I hold my incurable affections
up to a mirror. I watch an old man
panning the beach for treasure, a grass stem
bending under a blackbird.

Stirring and stirring cold coals in the fireplace,
remembering your white-shirred dress,
every rare morning like a porcelain cup.

—SAMN STOCKWELL (she/her)

CHANGE

If I go back and change everything when I was holding you
Then, suddenly, a force pushed me and took you away
And all I was left with was my empty hand.
Though time buried the memories, the moment
Flickers in the dark. Your twin innocent eyes still come
Every night. Is loss the bargain we make with God? Why does suffering
Remain so fresh? I can't save the loss. The books, the toys, the time,
The tracks were all lost. And you? You too lost track of time.
Certainly, I have the present. But who is living?
Each of us talks and eats together, but leaving.
What is left? Weary tracks
With buses honking to pick up the passenger for a ride.
At night, I hear many voices of crickets, dogs, and bats.
I still hear that distant hum of a broken song in the cold night.
I wish to touch it and mingle with that song forever.

—PULKITA ANAND (she/her)

I AM SUBTLE WITH MY SUFFERING

Instead of saying *suffocate me,*
I say *wrap your hands around*
my neck until I'm scarlet red.
Every so often, I step outside of my body
to witness my own demise.
I am audience and starring role—
and I always find a way to surprise myself.
I've been acting for as long as I can remember.
Acting happy. Acting in love.
Acting normal. Acting insane.
The velvet curtains close.
You look in love. You seem impressed.
I've fooled you once again.
Outside, the mid-summer air is thick and warm.
My thighs stick to each other like fresh meat
on bone and I think about turning myself
inside-out like a pair of old jeans,
revealing my imperfect hems, loose buttons,
and unstitched threads.
But I don't do that.
I am subtle with my suffering.
Instead of saying *I'm empty,*
I say *I'm hungry.*
I want your thumb in my mouth.
If my whole life has been one grand performance,
please, let this be my final one.
Lay me down in a bed of lilies and clover;
I want my satin skin scorched by the sun
because I only feel alive
when I'm burning.

—ANA DEE (she/her)

P AUL D ANO

I don't know how to talk to people anymore.
We're fucking in your yellow van.
You're still struggling to book roles and you're upset.
In our shoebox apartment,
we pretend we have a garden on our windowsill,
we have no water. We're in bed
and Paul, I'm sorry. Your movie L.I.E.
is in the bargain bin. A sorry is a knife.
We're in a vacant church, the saints are disappointed
in my head, the jokes are no longer funny.
We're so close to living in the alleyway.
We're drunk in a bar at the train station
as it's being gunned down
whatever you do, don't be a hero
put your hands up and don't make a sound.
I don't know what to do with my hands.
Gone so hard I can't walk

—D AVI S CHWEIZER (they/them)

OBEDIENT

I feel obediently erotic
he said eat so here I am in the kitchen
bending over more than I would if I wasn't
in a sheer nightdress with panties riding up wet pussy

Here I am lying on my bed but I'm
also on my knees & I can't stop imagining
what it would feel like to have a finger slipped in from behind
& an impact on my ass cheek

I have so much to do but I want someone to
care if I'm doing it
I want to be rewarded
I want to be a good good girl

I want an eye on me
I want to be held in place so I don't disappear
I want survival to feel less solitary & more like an exchange
I want to do more than survive I want to ejaculate

I want changing the sheets to feel necessary
I want to be something other than strong
they tried to switch me off so turn me on
my body is my body it's taboo but it's not wrong

—DEVON WEBB (she/her)

Ode to the Lesbian Lavender Haze

Free lilac or thick yellow***lavender menaces take to the street***devotion or
serenity

Flowers speak words we don't dare dream***in 1969***grace, calmness

Thin blue and long violet***The sweet floral scent***round white and tight black

Purity, silence***electrical suppressants keep it at bay***the vine, every soul

The best parts***Mediterranean native***Invasive beauty standards

Star stacked upon star***Forever reach but never grab***dead and buried

Woman catches woman's eye***gifts of sapphic interest***hidden beneath,

Flowers contained***whorls bound together***our spikes rise above the foliage

Endless rows of purple and gold beneath a blue sky***A gay little streak, a
dash***Numb it out

Bending***curving***reaching for the sky.

—SJ Larsen (they/them)

why i went back

won't you dance in the forest? please. slicing
open the spines of angels like a med-school
dropout, pressing confetti to the insides. send
me a heart. doesn't have to be yours. two and
three-headed lambs with ribbons around their
necks, pink and green and blue. in a dream i
strike you down, blade to the chest, and drag
it in a straight line across the length of your
body. a big orange snake with big orange
scales. i'm not done yet. last year, a wishing
star fell down the well and drowned,
electronics fizzling out as it sputtered, red
plastic-coated wires spooling out of it like guts.
don't know why i do what i've done.

what it felt like

let's speak in a language. plastic jeweled
hearts plastered over the walls. i have wings
and you would too if you'd just focus.
sequined and unlucky. neon pink and red and
black like roadkill. they threaded me into the
linings and won't let me out. shaking like a
dog. this is the last poem i'll ever write before
i write another one. the voices crowd the
riverbank. the carnival lights eclipse the
moon. please look for me in the ocean. say it.
would you promise? if i asked you to?

—ARYA VISHIN (he/him)

ABOUT RUNNING

There's a fantasy I have about running away
Been a mom since I was nineteen years old
Nineteen, just a baby myself

Responsible for another human all these years
Never a moment, for myself, about myself

I'd find somewhere small
With a diner in the center of town
Use an alias
Dye my hair

Go to bars in the middle of the day
Swim in lakes naked at night
Sleep till noon and write

There's a fear of wanting this too badly
My face nuzzled in the crook of her neck as she sleeps
Rubbing the sweat from her hairline
I weep into her pillow and beg forgiveness

These are the things you can't say out loud
I want to run away

Youngest crying again this morning
Oldest asking for her glasses to be cleaned
Milk falls from the counter
I trip over the dog
Were ten minutes late already

The moment they step from the car
I miss them, grab for them
I love you, I love you, I love you
They wave me silent

In the empty of the house
I shame my fantasy
Simmer in my awfulness
For wanting something other than them

—AZALEA AGUILAR (she/her)

about a woman with big feet:
she walks like a man.
Connected to her father by ambition,
her mother by apology,
too broad for her own good,
she'll walk all over you—
send a handwritten card.
She'll bust your ball and chain—
links only as strong
as her concealer. Her guilt, avoidance
of temptation when faced with bread basket—
her guilt, proportional to the circumference
of her wrist. Legally, she's required
to disclose: natural hair color,
thigh gap or wage gap,
number of men she's slept with—

—Cecilia Savala (she/her)

<u>INSTRUCTIONS</u>

Draw tally marks (or use the spiral method, if that's what you prefer) until your best friend tells you to stop. When they tell you to stop, try to nonchalantly sneak one more tally in, this is your future after all. If they catch you drawing one more line, protest! Say that its fate! This is what the universe wanted, this, and all the fake positivity that comes with it, *everything that happens, happens for a reason,* (abuse, stalking, sexual violence *[you are a girl after all—teehee],* or none of the above!) with the slip of your hand on the paper resulting in an extra line of ink! After the protest, get to counting[1]

M.A.S.H.

You will live in a....	Located in...	Married to...
Mansion.	Louisiana.	Aubrey Plaza.
Apartment.	Somewhere that will *almost* feel like home.	Harry styles.
Shack.	Arkansas (*oh god*).	Your high school boyfriend that you dated for purposeful reasons; the captain of the basketball team, the captain of the cheer team.
House.	A cold, cold, place.	He who Forced.
		A skater boy.

You will drive a...	You will have this many children...	You will have a career as a...
1993 stick shift Mercury Capri.	3.	Bartender, at the dive bar located down the block.
Hummer.	5.	Starving artist.
Motorcycle.	2.	Accountant (*many contexts implied, refer to TikTok*).
Pink Bug, an obnoxious one, with eyelashes nailed above the headlights.	8. 0 (*thank god*).	Doctor.

You will miss...	You will be...	Your hair will be...
The fights sometimes (*if we're being honest*).	Happy, happy (*happy?*).	Chopped off and donated, 14+ inches total.
Time with friends.	Filthy rich.	Long, to your ass.
Being able to go for a walk with headphones in.	Content.	Cut into a mullet (*finally*).
Drinking tequila, top shelf and bottom.	Sad, but in an okay way. Not sure if any of this is real.	Short, short-short, short enough to make He Who Forced text and say "every woman I've been with, has cut their hair off after sleeping with me".
Rest.		Copper-toned.

---

[1] If still confused on the instructions of this childhood game, Google it! Common'—get with the program! Tipity-tap "how to play M.A.S.H., a childhood game?" into the search engine—hurry! The future awaits!

My stomach hardens into a trunk.
I knock on it.   Hollow.   Bang.
Sprout two more arms like Kali Ma.
Branches crawl out of my back, skeletal wings.

Leaves spring from my scalp.
A bluebird tastes my hairline.
She squats, squeezes eggs.
I walk carefully
step   toe   step   toe
so as not to disturb her life-making.

I trek to the birch wood desk
at the end of the forest.
The light brown tree rings vibrate
when I sit in the chair,
my hands folded in the center,
obsidian crystal on my right,
gold wentletrap seashell on my left.

I flip over the shell and find
the Andromeda constellation pulsing,
a mollusk in search of water.
I drop the obsidian into the shell, wrench
two leaves from my hair, borrow
a song from the bird on my head.
The shell swallows it all up.

A pale white camellia flower blooms
from my navel, dressed in warm dewdrops.

—EVA LYNCH-COMER (she/her)

我长大的我想开心

we used to live by the kitchen clock, six minutes
early. the world would come to a halt if we
didn't. you would arrive early to pick
me up from national honor society and leave
ten minutes later. i would find my own way

home. like my ye ye did through a war, pressing
heel to toes until he lost count, until transience became a
state of being. he would learn the local dialects
in a day, chameleon himself into belonging. i wish
he would have taught me how to
turn every twist of tongue into a

home. instead we played solitaire, "just like life, most
of the time you don't win," in his teal blue corduroy
recliner. shuffling the paths we could have taken until
the suits blurred together and my plane flew

home. you would pick me up at the airport, departures
instead of arrivals so there was less traffic. you would
recount the "hate letters" i wrote you at 13–never mind
that i don't remember a single one. i made a list in 8th
grade of every person who had ever made me feel
small, you at the top, and in turn i forgave them
all, except for you. at 16, you would scoff at my
poems, call me dramatic, earn your place on
the list. at 27, you wouldn't read my first
poetry collection, the copy i brought

home for christmas dusty and spine un-
broken. i think all the times i wished on stray
eyelashes and coins in fountains, i just wanted
you to see me. how i walk for miles to
prove that i can, to turn coming

home into an accomplishment. how i cry at movies
and songs and moments, grieving a childhood
that broke me. how i carry my heart open

across oceans, and how i belong in cities
i've never been to: local shopkeepers greeting me in
chinese, wind on my face by the pacific, and every heart
break i've ever endured, soundless against the crash
of the waves. how my

home is everywhere and everyone i've loved, especially
when it was inconvenient. how i always run six minutes
late, and how the world spins anyway.

—KIERAN FU (they/them)

WE WENT ON A TRIP OUT OF TOWN THE SECOND TIME WE HUNG OUT AND I THOUGHT WE WOULD STAY FRIENDS FOREVER

I couldn't ask for
what I didn't know I needed.

      When I am dreaming,
      two different friends confess

love to me, heart locked.
I lean at my counter,

      coconut milk kale banana
      blending, dream of you.

I could have been silent as a mime,
your clown encyclopedia,

      held your hand through audits,
      avuncular confrontations.

Juggling truth and dream,
truth slipped

      from mouth a bag of groceries,
      soggy on cement.

Was it that you resembled Brando
but angry, more technical.

      My arms are full, in dreams,
      instruments, lyrics, drop cloths.

Distance vanishes feeling,
invisible like nutrition.

Paintings of whole families
at a free museum.

—**BROOKE HARRIES** (she/her)

HOW TO BE A GIRL

The girl at the top of her class, with waves
of chins and skin, *such a shame—*
a sugar shell, she sits like a man, moves
with purpose—she who's lost
and gained and lost. Still lost.

She avoids eye contact, accumulates
loose change. She who's underestimated,
converts T&A to ROI,
takes her own advice.

Like a man—whose mother
trained him to walk on the street side,
passed down handwritten recipes,
conserved water and nostalgia,
she makes bad news pretty.

She accepts compliments and memorizes
kitchen math to recite on command,
shares a room with divorce papers and cat hair.

—CECILIA SAVALA (she/her)

Arise from your unmade bed, glance out the window at the last sliver of night before dawn.

Remember the words someone spoke to you; *once you see, you can't unsee.*

Stumble blindly in the dark for some semblance of familiarity.

When you woke this morning, the world was tainted gold.

After months of blue haze, the ordinary takes on a life of its own.

The reflection in the mirror beams back at you, it's jarring.

Seeing yourself so happy.

Comb out your bedhead, begrudgingly brush your teeth, slide on your socks.

The car keys feel lighter in your hand, a smile cracks your lips.

Something's coming . . .

The cool October breeze bites your cheeks, a giggle bubbles up.

The commute is as it has always been, but that breeze clings to you.

Your air is still as the wind howls outside the car.

There is a quiet in your bones.

Your legs hobble beneath your weight.

No matter how you step, your stride has shifted.

Sit at your desk, everything slanted.

A faint clang as the fire within reignites and kicks back.

The first flicker of an ember in over a year.

Your skin crackles and pupils expand.

A second look at the desk in the fresh morning light.

Everything is exactly where it was meant to be.

Your vision burns as memory floods in vivid detail.

Warping under the piercing hot gaze of second sight.

The first pink hue seemed so innocent.
Each near hit, unwanted touch, verbal assault.

Her eyes had always burned crimson, you thought it was with passion.
She wanted to spin you into a waltz around hell.
So you took off the glasses and the world made sense again.

Tonight is the night you leave.

Once you see, you can't unsee.

—SJ LARSEN (they/them)

He Who Forced shows up on my social media feed—a TikTok. He's promoting his upcoming show, a concert at Peggy's—I roll my eyes and scroll. Begin watching the next video to pop up—then scroll back—he's wearing a gray-flannelled parka. His voice has changed, it's deeper than I remember—it rattles. I swipe out and open Facebook—his is still empty, desolate, wiped clean. The only thing his bio states is that he lives on the East coast now—my mind releases a scream.

He was home while I was home—we were both in the Midwest which reminds me of advice I once heard from an influencer—*driving down the interstate is the best time to scream*. Let me try it, I tell my partner. He doesn't understand that the best way to make a poem dated is by referencing TikTok. *So*, what am I supposed to do while my mind is spiraling—clean? Keep scrolling? I know it is coming soon—the rattle. He was home, in a gray-flannelled parka.

That damn parka. *The interstate is the best time to do it because you'll have the stereo blaring, bass bumping, space between cars to scream.* So, no one will be alarmed, they will be too focused on their morning commute to hear this rattle. My thumb on the steering wheel—feeling the leather, similar to how it feels on my screen when swiping through TikTok. He was home while I was home, he was home while I was home, he was home, I was home, he, I— I could write this until my fingers were riddled with carpal tunnel, upon a scroll. A new mantra forming (to repeat) while I clean.

That's what I do when I'm anxious—clean. Scrub floors with toothbrush, put in elbow grease, start a load of laundry, throw in a soiled parka. I'm sure I got this from my mother—us ladies, passing down quirky little traits through generations (teehee)—how to get through life by scrolling. Someone will eventually scream! Spoiler alert, it will be me because even cleaning the grout of our bathroom tile will make me think of a post I saw which will make me think of *THE* TikTok. You know the one by now—its echo a rattle.

Step out tonight at Peggy's—rattle—*ten-dollar cover*—rattle. I clean, I clean, I clean. Next door the church bells chime at the top of the hour, and hour, and hour—tick-tock. I cannot get it clean, this grimy fucking parka. To the car I go again, again, again, scream. Its sound—like the sound of the start of a clip after the start of the clip, ahEhGueCHWrSlHePLeas—as you scroll.

Stop—tell me I look pretty as I scroll. As I dance while I clean, baby, watch this ass rattle. Listen as I create music with my screams. I'm here baby, and I'm feeling clean! Watch me look elegant as I take out the trash, goodbye filthy parka! Hello Delusion, tell me that you've never seen a girl look so good as she slaps the wine bag, as she drops it low to wipe up dust, as she loses her phone so she can't find out He Who Forced is home, while she is home, on TikTok.

No, (a scream!) she lost her phone and didn't even look messy while doing it—now she can't even scroll! Forget Ke$ha, Mother of TikTok. Look at Cassandra brushing her teeth with a can of Mango White Claw–look at how good she ignores the rattle! She can do it all, drink and clean! A modern woman—living to forget the god-damn parka.

—ANNASTACIA STEGALL (she/her)

UNTITLED

stupid,   i hurricane around
your edges,   i turn left
on the wrong street,   say the wrong
things in the wrong order,   find myself
bleating,   find myself thinking things
in the wrong order,   staccato conversations
in which the phrase 'yeah,   but'
become the primary enemy,   i am
shorter than you today,   i am
inching towards your thighs,   in the
dress i didn't even get to wear,   that sat
limply in my suitcase,   that removed its own sequins,   butterflies
i am imprisoned,   i am in the city
i am walking down the alley,   i am
unbecoming when i'm like this,   key to the
back gate,   key to the
nostril,   a photo booth where
we could take pictures,   if you still
are in the city,   if i am still here
now

—maya cordero (she/her)

THE WORLD IS NOT A NATURE POEM

The world is in tilt
          moon brings out
          high tides and waves
          rush to overrun
          asphalt lots with kelp
          and sand.

When you look out into the horizon
          you won't see car
          fumes, grey puffs
          of poison   deep ocean
          fish stuck in
          sandy bottoms   tar
          gumming their gills   mercury
          filtrating through their
          bellies.

We are doomed to repeat
          patterns we didn't
          create   manufactured
          by the internal
          combustion engine.

We can't lay to rest
          our addictions. The world
          is a caterpillar

          in the sense that it will turn
          to deep sleep   chewing
          at leaves   chewing
          at our interiority   gnawing
          away at our conscious
          thoughts.

It doesn't matter
         that a butterfly will one day
             emerge   the poisons
             have already been digested.

—CARLA SCHICK (they/them)

How I yearn to nuzzle close and clutch you tight—
My beloved, desecrated, disgraced mother tongue.
With bare palms I will wipe your coarse crust,
with tongue-tips I will lick your hoarse wounds,
then anoint the bruises—your proud, buried emblems.

Many nights we nestled beneath the blinking stars,
duets scribbled on diary lines and textbook margins,
letting your bones and my vulnerable vessel
together uphold the splendor of memory gold,
and unleash the long-crouched wildness
to crash into splinters of somniloquy and song.

Tonight, I will stitch my ache into ribs once more,
with two kinds of needles where sorrow and spark crisscross,
allowing your butterfly's shadow to thread
through my snow-lashed ridge,
until the inner roar cresting in whitecap
thumps into an upright spine of courage.

Perhaps lurking in life's hushed ravine,
I've long awaited a current of revelation—a tide-borne oracle
to arouse the ancient flood hibernated in my blood.
Before it wells up and breaches my chest,
from a throttled throat I will cry out—
"Mama, Mama."

—Celia Lan (she/they)

CAVE PAINTINGS

Cave paintings flicker in my consciousness
Where aurochs groan and rumble
Across a sleepy Earth,
Woolly rhinoceros poses for a portrait
So everyone will know
We lived together.

In the sheltering passages
I see the women
Singing while they are sewing,
Finishing up the paintings,
Giving the dead man an erection.

Cave paintings flicker
In the part of my heart
That cradles lust for life.
We were there, we were there!
And then I awake
To this distant, broken dream,

—JENNY MCBRIDE (she/her)

A Bronco, Bolivia, Y Nosotros

There isn't a corner in Cochabamba where you can't see the mountains
They seem to call on you as witness

Both our families herded cattle over foothills
Walked miles, dirt roads, rocks in their shoes for school
Knelt over maíz, penance for sins

They say Lake Angostura once stretched the whole of this valley
You and your sister remember taking row boats to reach Arbieto

Roads are paved now, a new one each time you visit
Giant art deco houses for miles that don't match the landscape
Your father tells us they belong to los americanos

Locals have begun staking ownership
Building small wooden huts along the mountain side

Who does it belong to?
Spaniards stole it first you say
Left it abandoned
It belongs to no one now

Your father points to the casa of his abuela
Who had fig trees
All the grandkids would come for its fruit he chuckles

We travel to Tarata for their chorizos
Stop in Cliza for chicharrón
Made in giant discos on the street

Women sell baby rabbits, ducks in cages
Awwww Sophia screeches
Para comer her Tia offers
Her eyes open widely in silence

We make offerings to Pachamama
Items thrown into the fire
Requests for *amor, salud, más hijos*
Está cerrado I shout!
Everyone laughs
I can be funny in Spanish

Your sister shows me all the land your grandma owned, her mothers
before her

It was the women in this family who held power, in mine too

We visit the adobe house in Liquinas where all the children were born
Two died during childbirth
Nine total your father says
All girls before him, his father hungry for a boy

I weep as we say goodbye
Wish for a way to stay

When you ask why I love it here
I fumble with explanation
Tempo, texture, people lips dark as plum
Everyone looks like your father, like you

There is an us that dreams rest here
Allows quiet, laughter, finds family, each other

—AZALEA AGUILAR (she/her)

SILVER SHOES

Anticipating an intruder—always—I entered.

I caught him like a taxi, or a flu.

This whole notion that something will shake out.

The wind spreading seed and pollen and mingling parts of plants
unsayable. Pretty manipulative if you think about it.

I pounced on the last feasible haircut appointment.

The birthday I insisted on a candle for every year,
the waitress was appalled by my self-advocacy,
that I could fret over my own cake.

Another year, the server said I looked my age.
I don't understand time or age,

unless it means one year compared to another.
This year is going by fast. I feel eleven
or a lucky seventy-one some nights.

I could never be indifferent. I would like to hunt
for something to praise in consumerism,
debt systems, hostage-making debris.

The silver shoes became ruby slippers.
When I finally saw *The Wizard of Oz*, it was too late;
I was no longer a child.

Under the right spell already so Hollywood couldn't find me,
I read books selected by a bookstore worker named Leif—

Stood a little out of line
to bring them into my shortlong life.

—BROOKE HARRIES (she/her)

Sometimes I grow tired of being
the softness I begged for,
then I fall asleep

before they do, surrounded by
an ever-growing exhibition
of popsicle sticks glued into
sculptures that scare them
at night. I dream

of Rapunzel's hair, a golden waterfall
long enough for them to hold on to
in their sleep while I crawl
into my own bed on the second floor.

I pack fruit into their bags
like offerings to gods
who may or may not
believe in me. At school,
they shed their skin—undershirts
I insisted on, manners, my
unlived lives. I let them win

but not always. They leave
fingerprints on every surface
of my life. I swallow my storms
to make room for their weather.
They borrow my scarves and
my voice, rarely return them
unaltered. I guess that's the point:

Rehearsing the absence—
the minute they leave our skin.
I leave the hallway light on.
Just in case.

—TANJA LAU (she/her)

THE ORANGE PEEL THEORY

Crisscrossed, I sat on the cold tiled floor,
beneath my grandmother, in the living room.
Enveloped in her floral bata, grey hair braided
and thrown over her shoulder, gold-rimmed
glasses, locked into concentration.

My hands stretched out, waiting for the peel to fall
into my palms. In awe, watched each time. This was
magic to me.

I knew not to move, had been taught, this required
patience, the blade somehow, dull enough
not to pierce her thumb, yet sharp enough to cut
across the sometimes-stubborn fruit.

I can no longer remember her voice. She was not
the type of woman to shower us with I love you's. Yet
each time, she appears between the small mist of an
orange ruptured by the blade.

At the grocery store, she hovered over the produce
display, going over each navel orange before putting
it into the plastic bag, and before moving away she
taught my mother how to peel an orange with as much
of the rind still attached.

Today, I am in love with a Puerto Rican woman. When
packing her lunch, this morning I plucked a mandarin,
from a Halo's bag, inspected closely before buying.

I break into the small fruit with my thumb, separating
each segment, delicately rubbing the rind off the
surface, picking the pith off each slice because
she doesn't like the feeling of string in her mouth.

I was taught, to be Puerto Rican, isn't to simply
say I love you with everything in me. Its

standing at the kitchen counter, waking up 5
minutes before your alarm goes off, insuring
only perfection for her fruit.

The Ziplock bag filled with my love carried by her for the rest of her day.

—CHANICE CRUZ (she/her)

These learned burdens grip
like thorns,
half-fresh grief that lasts
an eternity.

We wait for answers
from the future, but will
we heed the blood
of the vanished?

Their absence builds
like water,
stones succumbing to pressure
and convulsed laughter.

—ELENA LUCIA PEREZ (she/her)

GENTEEL GASH

Loving you
was a reality
check and tick
of everything that
kills me, the crater
murmuration of all the
millions of pins you stuck
in my skin, the list goes on
and on and on and let's repeat
for clarity's sake, ha, one more for
the impact, as if it would dry the tears
I spent loving you when you were not worth
it, blinded by your quest for random obscurity
confused it with love, oh I was so starved and I
lost track of time and self and sanity, and now when
all is said and done, even when your apparition constricts
my sternum, what I am in the end is dreadfully, mindnumbingly
bored of your cowardice, I once thought you were a mirror and fell
for the long list of things that now make the skin that longed for you
crawl, every item a blow to my very soul, how could you, how can you
who even are You, how do you walk around in a patchwork skin suit collage
of personas of the suckers you cracked open and left, on to the next mystery
while I, your brutalized monster, balance the weight of your genteel soft gashes

—PHAEDRA SAFFRON (they/them)

Tutti Frutti
—after all the names they gave me

Six fruits,
    some I bit,
        some bit me.
Sugar over rot,
    souring
        beneath my tongue.

He said I smelled like guayaba,
    ripe, rusted,
        pulga-market trace.
Whispered it inside me,
    in the dark,
        siempre en sombra
            never en sol.
Words clung, dusk on skin,
    a rind torn back
        by memory.

I tasted the lie,
    spat the seed
    into hollow,
Let it rattle in my teeth,
    hard as a no.

Saw my tongue
    on durazno,
        gold fuzz electric,
            a dare, a curse.
No seas joto.
Juice an insult,
    sliding, stinging,
        down my chin.

I kissed higo,
    soft, morado.
        Dios está mirando
            (he said).

Syrup in his palm,
    wiped on church boletín.
My mouth sticky
    with God and guilt,
violet as confession.

Toronja,
    bitter, sharp.
I returned
    to bite again.
Citrus never scabs.
Acid bright,
    wounds caustic
        when I smile.

Zapote,
    dark, demasiado.
Me tragó.
    Laughed:
    "Didn't count, bro.
        Just us."
His laugh, acrid,
    a pit I roll
    between molars,
        I refuse to swallow.

One cholo:
    "Esa tuna se abrió, güey."
Let him taste
    floral notes,
        already peeled.
Espinas,
    gloquios,
        sabor.
My skin burst, cactus-bloom,
    floral and feral.

Let him drink deep,
     let him bleed
          if he must.

They called me
Tutti Frutti.
So I wore it,
     head high,
     tongue bitten,
crown of pulp and peel,
     walking the market
          like a dare.

Now they bite
     their tongues.
Their fruit rots
     behind closed teeth.

I open my mouth,
     name every fruit,
          seed by seed.
Spit what is left,
     let it root
          in the cracks they made—
my tongue sprouting thorns from pulp,
orchard unruly, unkept,
          mine,
               never theirs

—JAIME RODRÍGUEZ (he/him)

HOW SUMMONING SOMETHING BECOMES ROUTINE / HOW TO SCREAM
OUT OF BODY / HOW SOME RELIGION WILL SAY IT'S POSSESSION

THIS REQUIRES ME TO BE LAMBASTED WITH DISTORTION
            SKIN SHIMMYING WITH GRAY GLITTER SO WET AND GNASHING

where is the origin of pain that diffracts me? but, diffract as in light that cannot penetrate dirty summer inflatable pool water dosed with spheres of chlorine in a last-ditch attempt to save it from inevitable autumn? how the algae stagnates in this phantasmagoric liquid like atoms refusing to split under a microscope, until it must? how the fracturing is not only a prediction, but an expected occurrence in scientific processes? how did the hypothesis not consider human error inflicted by others, and a shifting as a tool of recovery?

AM I LESS HUMAN AND MORE SPIRAL OF STATIC
                            LIKE A SNAKE EATING ITS TAIL
OR PAISLEYNOISE
            A DECONSTRUCTION OF WHIMSY AND PROTECTIVE TEXTURE?

–tommy wyatt blake (he/they)

The ______ and He Who ______ met at a party that He Who ______'s
   NOUN   VERB   VERB

best friend, invited The ______ to. The ______ wanted more than anything
                         NOUN   NOUN

for someone to look at her and be able to tell she had lived, even though

she hadn't lived much. So, to the party she went. All night long they sat next

to a roaring bonfire and talked about Camus and Kafka and how her copy

of The Stranger was bath-ridden and coffee-stained, dog-eared a plenty.

It was ______ in other words. Of which The ______ wanted it to so
        VERB   NOUN

desperately be, because love meant protection. She yearned for ______,
                                                 NOUN

a body sleeping next to her to keep the rattling noises at bay. So, The

______ laughed at all of He Who ______ jokes and he, likewise, continued
NOUN   VERB

to ______ absurdism to The ______. It was a match made in ______,
   VERB   NOUN   NOUN, A PLACE

chatting as they watched the fire soften from rage to finally, rest.

Months later, The ______ drove a drop top, with a hole sliced through the
                   NOUN

middle that had spawned from a tiny tear. The creation story goes as

follows: He Who ______ thought the tear looked like a ______ and began
              VERB   NOUN

working fingers through without permission, until a fist was through fabric

in his wake. The ______ watched in ______ as fingers went in one by one,
           NOUN   ABSTRACT NOUN

leaving the tear wide and frayed. Strings tangling in the wind as she drove,

unsure of how to make themselves whole again.

Before the creation of the hole, she got a flat tire on the interstate and after

calling everyone in her contact list, The ______ thought to call He Who
                                          NOUN

______. Sure, she had just met him last week, but he had mentioned how
VERB

he lived nearby this side of an unfamiliar town. He gladly accepted and she,

taking shelter from the wind, decided to wait in her lovely beater named

Bub, for her knight in ______ armor to arrive. In which he did. Followed by
ADJECTIVE

trying to exhaustively loosen the bolts to her tire. Eyes wide (what she

would later know as his ______ eyes) and searching, the moon shone on
ADJECTIVE

every individual curl of hair his hair, giving it life, animation, recoil, to help

push. This is the specific moment when The ______ fell in love, not with
NOUN

He Who ______, but Who She Dreamed Him to Be. He tried to loosen the
VERB

bolts to no avail. They were stuck there, stranded and flailing, for a year

and a half.

Generative Word Bank For if Stuck and Need Help

NOUN
Content, Glass, Prude, Heaven, Vagina, Horror, Hell, Rain, Boy, Garden, Bed, Vixen, Desire
VERB
Followed, Listened, Mansplain, Accept, Encourage, Longing, Frighten, Kneel, Love, Offend, Preserve, Forced
ADJECTIVE
Happy, Careful, Dirty, Jealous, Shining, Crazy, Helpful, Smiling, Joyous, Troubled, Cruel, Fine

**Inspired by Mad, a poem by Jane Wong*

trust is fighting a losing battle with the present

a moment is precarious,
in an instant the candle catches the dress on fire
a gunshot rips through your shoulder as the doctor
says gently that you won't live to see the end of the year.
we broke up while i was in the hospital
it's still a lesser evil, compared to what my body
was trying to put me through.

a morning text chain in my family group chat reads
ice drove past my school in a van
it's probably fearmongering
though the rumor is they're heading to the high school
it's graduation day, there'll be
more parents there.

a man smiles at his son
all lips and teeth as they are torn apart
it's okay, he says though he doesn't believe it
the son nods, though he doesn't believe it
that's the last they'll see of each other
headed towards unknown futures of someone else's creation.

this needs to stop
the chorus rings out but the vans
keep driving

the street vendor washes out the eyes
of people sprayed with tear gas
with the milk he bought for his aguas frescas

this is wrong, the community shouts
the wrong continues so now it's
part of everyday life in the
world we live in.

people lock their doors, they
stop going to work,
stop going to court.

tucked into the strap of their bras,
they carry an ever growing list of places they can
no longer go.
last week the block was an arioso of
reggaeton, corridos, and the laughter
of a grandmother being proved right.

today it's so quiet
you can hear the sirens going off in
everyone's heads.

one lock clicks shut,
then another. if anyone asks
nobody's home.

—CATHERINE SHONACK (she/her)

Snow Angels in Virginia

On Dec 2009, it snowed in Virginia.
The flight I was supposed to be on
got delayed. When snow falls in Virginia
everything stops. Snow as a miracle.
Uncle Kenny, who towered over us all,
eyes sparkled in the bright white sky,
he ran over to his thin brown jacket,
Ma grabbed the closest skully to her
which probably belonged to Marcus.
They opened the thick red door
and we all felt so lucky.

It's 2009 in December, time is falling
from the sky. My pilot checks his phone,
we are all on standby, as Ma and Uncle
Kenny's laughter cuts through the chilled
air, parts of their smiles still somewhere
in Brooklyn in the 80's. Sissy and I are
seeing them whole. Uncle Kenny runs to
the side of the house to gather a supply
for our snowman, We haven't seen a white
November since our last winter in Queens.
Ma throws herself on the ground, she is
making snow angels in our front yard. Sissy
jumps off the porch into a pile, her eyelashes
sparkle as the white dust rises around her.

In 2009, it snowed in Virginia, we
somehow got more time. We barely
had enough for our malnourished
Snowman, who pronounced words
like scrimp. Simply because we are
at least for the moment, proud to call
ourselves Virginians, though even
sissy still got that New York thick
skin. We make do with what we got.

We, all smiles at the offering from the
sky.

In 2009, in my next lifetime, I want nothing
more than to be the snow angel beneath
my mother's back during a sad snowstorm
in Virginia.

—CHANICE CRUZ (she/her)

i.

I dream,
decades into the future,
of holding my thambi's
dead body.

I press my hand to his chest, I say:
Show me what you were made of.

My hand becomes a knife, and
I cleave his skin.
Beneath his ribs lies
a sphere of gold
smattered with streaks
of pink and orange—

a sunset for a soul.

I bring the blade further down,
and within his stomach, I find
a swing set. The structure is home
to two kids stretching out their feet,
reaching for the sky.

Thambi, chinaiyya,
I remember it too.

ii.

The funeral day has come and gone.

A hole in the earth, dug
in a field of wildflowers,
was his passageway.

As the sun begins to match his soul,

I lay across his grave,
and I sing to him.

He hears me, I know.

I sing to him
our childhood songs, all
the tunes our appa loved.
I sing until the sun
goes into hiding and
the stars give us company.

Beneath their glow,
I pluck a wildflower
growing flush to his grave
and begin walking home.

iii.

Miles and miles pass
until I reach
a street with a lonely swing.

I seat myself on the leather, wildflower
still held tight between my fingers, and I

launch us into the air—
reaching for the sky.

—CYPHER (she/her)

The beginning of Rilke's elegies,
a subtle headache coming.
For dinner, I'll complain.

It must be love,
can't look directly at it.
And I feel like being economical,
can't tell you
the pain of looking at your picture.

All I could say folded, hidden.
Like that sun on the hillside,
sky at dusk and just after.
Needing you isn't a bow drawn across strings.

I want you like a dream I woke from,
confident nothing broke in the night.
The branch that fell on the scar
on the windshield didn't hurt the glass.

—BROOKE HARRIES (she/her)

Exhale

She says she's never smoked
a cigarette but would like to,
the way one says

    the grass could use a good rain
    or *I would like to try tiramisu someday*

      —unrushed and under her breath.

This is what resignation looks like:

    the long drag of an exhale—
      a slippery slope
        that, at some point,
          plateaus.

We look around for a god or light or mirror—
anything we can hold ourselves up to.

—NICHOLAS OLAH (he/him)

You memorized the saddle of my hips under my mother's.
Between the linens & the languid limbs of moonlight slotting through. Shades.
Of navy cosmos, silt and humiliation.
Wolves' gab and giddy banter, swallowed by my. Over plates of modest
Fare. You praised me with. Indignation & heat cravings. On a plateau of oak slats
& floated ego. Writ of invitation to the faceless mountain a decade has. Parents'
folly drowning out our. Hands reigning hands.
Let us slosh a milk pearl between us both. Ritual stitched to the palms of our hands,
Slices of our lips, we are without the juvenile unknowing.

—LORENA MARIA (they/them)

I hated anything falling in the shower. What if all my important patterns turned out to be coincidences? Meaningless. Like inexplicable sink water. The full fog of years I spent sidestepping reality, sleeping on couches in the shadows of self-actualized people with penchants for hiking. People sleeping outside. Angel Island sitting there. Cat said I was too busy to work. A recession. Historically, earthquakes caused mostly fire damage. I misremembered a California children's book about the earthquake of 1906. At the Winchester Mystery House, thought of my mother, not guns or peoples. Ghosts disorient still; an all-denim outfit deranges me, recalls my uncle in jail posed with his friends in the yard grinning confidently. An idiot, I thought. A local skateboarder was smitten with me before I moved. One night, parked outside the Legion of Honor Museum in his Miata, I asked why. He said because the picture of your uncle in jail. Memories ruin my poems. Oh! When he first texted days in a row, he wrote I didn't mean to sink so fast. The little poem of it sent me awhile.

—**BROOKE HARRIES** (she/her)

WOMAN CAUGHT IN STORM

In your palms, you offer me
a picturesque future: *think suburbia,*
think picket fence, think school-zone,
think engagement ring—a future
where you save me from myself.
As a master of self-destruction,
I find pleasure in the way
my body bends when pushed
by forces outside of its control,
like how earlier today,
I decided to take a stroll
in the middle of a storm—
below zero with no coat,
just a sultry sundress,
the wind whipping my wet hair
in every direction, pellets
of freezing rain sticking
to my exposed thighs
and striking my cheeks
like an old-fashioned slap in the face.
I imagine this moment becoming
a headline on the 6 o'clock news:

> WOMAN CAUGHT IN STORM.
> *Where was she headed? Nobody knows.*

All I know is I am leaking sadness
all over the place. In your palms,
you claim you hold the key to happiness—
though I never asked to be saved,
rather, quite the opposite:
I wanted to be destroyed.

—ANA DEE (she/her)

SEE HOW MUCH I LOVE YOU?

I keep all your
fingernails in a jar.
When I'm sad, I open
the lid and rake
through the clippings.
In this way I feel
how deep my love goes,
how many unthanked
tasks I perform to groom
and feed you. I keep all
the songs I've sung you,
I thread them through
your cells.
Can you hear them
singing you to sleep?

—JESSICA BATES (she/her)

Homesick

power goes off in the middle of the night
water comes in slow drips from rusty faucets
fridges offer moldy cheese and rotten milk
humidity weighs heavy on your chest
I climb tree tops, imagine faraway places
where the air isn't so salty
at nineteen with a newborn
Grandma squeezes hard, makes me promise
"Mija, don't you ever come back,
never come back, entiendes?"
so much love in losing
my sister sends money for a uhaul
you can't raise this baby there baby
decades later, news is constant
girlfriends who I smoked weed with on the gulf
stared at stars with, from pickup trucks
needles in their arms
shot by guns they bought for lovers
their children left behind
I knew them before, when we tried
to get lost on roads we memorized

—Azalea Aguilar (she/her)

97

p.s. i hope you write me back

weapons aren't just blades, knives and swords
they're eyes that throw glances
sharp enough to cut through your ego

make you think of the ruins you've created

weapons are words we don't swallow
that we allow to come up
through the broken and cracked pipes
that might burst with emotion

weapons are moving towards
uninhabitable lands filled with toxins
designed to kill the human spirit

let the bullets stay in their barrel

impress me with a song
that fills generations with sorrowful thought

show me how to weaponize
freedom
into a
revolution

what is a dream
when breath is unmanageable

the boot you told me to pick myself up by
is crushing my neck

the intricate imprints of the tread
paint my skin in hues of red

i guess it's just
something to remember you by

a love letter from a nation

—ALEXIS RAYMOND (she/her)

IT WAS THE MOST UNINSPIRED BENDER I'VE EVER BEEN ON IN MY LIFE, NEARLY TWO WEEKS STRAIGHT JUST HALF FUCKED ON MOLLY, COKED OUT, ROLLING AROUND IN BED WITH THE TV ON, GILMORE GIRLS AND THE SOUND OF SHEETS TURNING OVER,

BUT THERES NO USE CRYING OVER SPILT SYNAPSES, CHEMICAL DEPENDENCIES, TOMORROWS DEPRESSION,

WHICH CAN ONLY BE FACED TOMORROW, WHICH CAN NOT BE ALLEVIATED TODAY,

TODAY, 10,222 DAYS AFTER THE ASSASSINATION OF BENITO MUSOLLINI, I AM WRITING YOU TO ASK IF MAYBE I'VE BEEN MISGUIDED, IF MAYBE THERE IS, ANOTHER USE FOR A LENGTH OF ROPE

—maya cordero (she/her)

Previously published in Midcult

How to un-sex yourself.
Unbrand the mournful lips & yet entrench pleasure

How to flatten the chest.
Your perpetually pitiful breasts, like the bulging eyes of a small dog

How to shave the subtle swell of your hips.
Caving bone that mingles with scaffolding of the ribs

How to apportion your silhouette in noon light
Peace treaty with the limits of mortal creation

How to array a beloved in splendor
& enmesh our veins into a trembling pact

—LORENA MARIA (they/them)

she / her / hers
millennial fight
to own a pronoun
not dominated by
he / him / his

buy into the wreck
up / over / beyond
this new deep well
they / them / theirs
unmoored plenitude

abolishing every
bullshit binary (we wish)
and we're back in bed
with the rationalists
(best we've got)

wishing, dreaming
will and intellect
would be one

—DION FARQUHAR (she/her)

How to Be a Girl

I make amends, and you,
sawdust outlines, non-alcoholic drinks.

I make boilerplate references to sepia-toned violence,
keep medical records to myself.

Manuals insinuate the way it's always been,
underripe more satisfying than overdeveloped.

Consider the *amuse-bouche*,
the before picture.

I like my girls like I like my barbecue:
thick and sweet, a little bit messy,

girls who tend gardens of eyebrows,
go to bed early, drink their breakfasts.

—CECILIA SAVALA (she/her)

fern-throat

the forest tilts
    as if listening
    for a wound

I press my cane into soil
   and the ground exhales—
     a hollow ribcage
    beneath me

the creek shivers
   stones spit out their names

I kneel where ferns gather
   their green throats
      open wider than mine

silence is not empty
    it is a mouth
      holding everything back

roots climb the air
   with questions
I cannot answer

so I stay—
   long enough
    for shadow to notice

long enough
   for the wind
    to take my breath
     and return it burning,
    cracked

—KATH HEALING (they/them)

monotony. reiterations of the commonplace a
unawareness leaving behind ghost prints that g
change. analogous to a monotype drawn on
execution of a second, renounces an apparition
erroneously reproduces portions of the prece
and overlapping residues confine those once-
resistance cannot undertake—within the tangi
a dispersive motion: a person being progressed
immovable apparatus, can only retreat in though
to counteract the inevitable through abductive
rules, rooms, ceilings, people, objects, things, ha
for sustaining equilibrium among humans here,
that was finally remembered after some time, fla
stray dog in the nearby park,

a neat incision, like the head I dissected, all split
nerves, circulatory, cardiovascular: sacculina th

lways unfold subtle mutations in a stillness of
radually drift, becoming anchor points initiating
smooth surfaces like glass. a first print, then
-like, elusive grayscale image. similarly, a printer
ding page onto the following. the faint, blurry,
mirages — ghost images that materials of low
ble. the surroundings skim over, advancing in
forward in a state of stasis, being bound to an
t through flashbacks, backstepping, attempting
reasoning. a sudden semibreve rest.
bits, routines, modes of operation, principles
layout of the kitchen, arrangement of spices
me heights from each stove, tree and grass, the

open from the middle, continuously fracturing;
ings: clear, return to zero.

—TRACY CHENXI SHI (she/her)

Magnolias Beneath the Rain

The utter act, the utter pleasure of anticipation,
of waiting, of counting the days to Sunday,
when Saturday extended hour by hour, moment by moment,
lengthened, straightened, tightened to the thinnest waif—
it was pleasure singed with pain, it was breath taking flight,
it was aqua and emerald rolled to waves, crossing
those verdant paths, beneath magnolias, dripping rain,
descending, descending, to the rushing blackwater
for an hour, only an hour, once a week—
breath on breath, skin on skin,
words useless, empty, meaningless, for my eyes
had been scouting yours in the preceding hours, sometimes to be found.
Now, the light has returned, piece by piece. It is an ending,
twisted to size, twisted to my shape.

—SARAH DALY (she/her)

FICTION

Almost immediately, I notice Jamie doesn't have any clothes on in my dream. I'm in my own garden, but it is a small, flat area divided into sections by low, whitewashed walls. The sky is overcast and has sucked the colour out of everything. I am digging in the soil with a pointed trowel, loosening the roots of a stubborn weed. Our neighbour, Jamie, begins conversation in his usual, halting phrases of practiced congeniality. After knowing him for some years, I wonder if it's an affectation, a manufactured pace (just-a-beat-behind) to make his own thoughts more winsome. He will often employ the word "indeed" to agree with a point that's been made. He also has the habit of rhetorically repeating the one-word question, "Right? Right?" Yet despite being intermittently emphatic, exchanges are dull with this man whose sympathetic eyes belie understanding. Instead, the furrow in his brow and nod of his head are gestures of evolution's work in camouflage. What does a predator really want? In polite company, I can't ask. Manners and other social protocols prevent me from being so direct.

In my dream garden, Jamie is confident and parades his nakedness around as if to shock me into being comfortable with his pale bulk. I look up at him to take in his full form. My dismay and disgust pivot quickly. This man has no protection against any harm I can inflict.

***

Last month on my birthday, Jamie presented me with a bottle of expensive rosé. A gift from him and his beautiful wife. There was no one else in the living room. I was holding the bottle, as he towered over me showering me with superficial accolades in a declarative tone full of verve. He squeezed my shoulder, slapped the side of my bare thigh hard with his open palm, and gestured like a showman in a piece of garish theatre.

Then he went quiet. Did I hear? A neighbour's child had fallen gravely ill. Fever. Seizures. Unconscious. Jamie kept rubbing his chin. The scratch of his five o'clock shadow against his hand produced a grating sound. I waited for a pause.

"You know what?" I asked.

He looked at me earnestly. Perhaps he assumed we would commiserate over the sick child. Perhaps he readied himself for an embrace in which he could offer tenderness to ward off any frantic maternal panic. In my ear, he'd whisper reassurances and the necessity of gratitude for the good health that blesses both of our families.

"Yes?" A single word, a soft hiss, imploring my affection.

"You know when you touch me? When you slap me?" Jamie locked eyes with me. The muscles in my face visibly tightened. "I don't like that."

Over the years, I rigged up a deadly, make-believe, Wile E. Coyote pulley system that swung over Jamie's head whenever we met. It is a simple mechanism: a large rock suspended by a string that I held. I pulled the string higher every time he rubbed me too low on my back, insisted on feeding me food, grabbed and held me too close in an impromptu dance move. On my birthday, I gave myself a present: I finally let go of the string and dropped the rock. No one was physically hurt, but it broke the floor and I could have sworn dust floated up around us. My heart leapt and I had to stop myself from smiling.

"I'm sorry." That same gentle hiss, but said far too quickly.

"You've done that before. You've touched me before and I don't like it."

I spun on my heel and left him, his gaping face so unaccustomed to this kind of worry.

***

In my dream, we are engaged in a heated argument. Jamie is no longer apologetic. He is defensive, accusing me of being oversensitive, of deliberately destroying our relationship. He wants me to cherish the times our families went camping together, the dinner parties we shared amongst the company of our adoring spouses and close friends, the eager help he offered when my husband wasn't well. He wants to be reinstated as a good man and a good friend. He wants me to renounce all offenses and grant him full clemency.

His defense turns angry. He has marched over the low walls between us and moved closer to where I am standing in the garden, his naked heft no more appealing than what hangs in an abattoir.

Suddenly, I am on him. Surprised, he stumbles. His back flattens against a brick wall. The sharpened trowel in my hand sinks into the side of his flesh. I shove it in as hard as I can but doubt the force of my own strength. I cannot cause the harm I want. I cannot, with the strength of my own hands, kill him—not even in my dreams.

109

***

When I wake, I wonder if Jamie is really injured. Perhaps there's been an inconsequential mishap. Maybe a fall while riding his bike? Or a slip of a knife while making dinner? I desperately want to ask my husband to reach out and check how he is. But I can't. Such an unusual request would prompt suspicion and I would be compelled to explain myself. How can I be certain that my version of Jamie's indiscretions would be accepted without question?

Especially now that I am a woman who has been caressed and full of distress? The moment I disclose his hand touched my body, I will become a woman to loathe.

Instead, the wife calls.

Have I heard? Mark and Barb's little boy is OK two nights in the hospital and all the tests came back clear what a relief we should celebrate Jamie bought a bouquet of flowers and a card a really nice card you guys are welcome to sign it too by the way happy belated birthday did you try the wine of course Jamie and I only drink red but thought you'd love it are you and hubby free tonight I know it's last minute but Jamie has been making dynamite rolls all afternoon and there's no way we can eat all of them ourselves we have another bottle of your birthday rosé chilling in the fridge hold on a sec . . .

I hear Jamie talking in a low tone to her in the background.

Hi hi again are you still there Jamie wanted you to know that he just scored a Bob Marley album Kaya we can't believe the condition M-I-N-T Jamie won't tell me how much he paid for it "I feel so good in my neighbourhood" you're the best neighbours so come over OK? after 8 OK?

I didn't realize it at the time, but the violence in my dream was being recorded. Once this phone call ends, the film is set aflame. The motion of my hand twisting against Jamie's flank is the last scene in a series of single, blinking frames. Before Jamie begins to bleed, black edges of the film curl onto our orange flesh and our pain melts under erratic, toxic heat. My dream escapes into ash.

***

All dreams are cinematic. Our minds are masterful cinematographers specializing in spinning truth from threads of the incongruent and absurd. Asleep, we are all protégés of the surrealist master, Dali.

***

With an invitation so enthusiastically extended, I tell my husband that we dare not decline to partake in Jamie's handmade dynamite rolls and rosé. I tell him about Bob Marley and my husband gets excited. He starts singing "Wake up and / Wake up and / Wake up and / Turn I loose / For the rain is falling."

We agree we cannot go empty handed. My husband rushes to pack a cooler of half a dozen IPAs because he knows Jamie won't tolerate more than one glass of the rosé. He scoffs. Slightly.

Almost like a cough to clear his throat. The sound alarms me. Is he mocking Jamie or is the pink drink too sweet? Too effete? A little jeer to jab the little dear? My husband refuses to drink rosé.

I tell him I'll take some impatiens from the garden and put them in a pot for Jamie and his wife. All my touch-me-nots are bright pink, the colour of an open, screaming mouth.

***

My husband has put on a light jacket and announces he's ready to go. I am washing my trowel with dish soap in the kitchen sink. He asks what the hell I'm doing. I can't think quickly enough to come up with a reasonable answer. I feign confusion, "Garden tools. Knives and forks. Force of habit. I wish we had a dishwasher." He mutters that I better not have clogged the sink with dirt. The trowel shines after I dry it with a dish towel. I press its tip into my open palm until the skin looks kissed by a stigmata. I don't let my husband see me slip it into my purse.

The fading memory of my dream sings from behind the garden wall. Its voice is disappointed and tired. The shame it incites goads me on to fulfill an operatic destiny.

***

We're half-way out the door and the wife calls again.

Oh my god the ambulance just left I'm going to the hospital now I can't believe it it happened so fast Jamie was on a step stool reaching for the good wine glasses he wanted to use the crystal ones for you guys you know how he likes to make things nice and we're celebrating right? right? he slipped and hit his back on the edge of the opposite counter you know he's a big enough guy

111

and gave himself a good blow he couldn't feel his legs so the paramedics think it might be a nerve thing oh my god oh my god i gotta go . . .

I offer to drive her to the hospital, but she wants to go by herself. So, I promise to call her in the morning.

***

That night, I dream I have lost something in my garden. There are no flowers, trees, or bushes. Soft, dark soil covers the entire space. Kneeling on the ground, I am digging with my bare hands. Even with so much effort, I am only unearthing more earth. I abandon one spot for another, and then, another. The soil senses my desperation and begins to undulate and bubble. This makes me nervous, so I dig faster until I hit something sharp. I recoil and look at my hands. Shiny metal tips are emerging from each of my dirty palms. The blood pouring out floods the garden.

—JOYLYN CHAI (she/her)

My friend Connor thought he knew a lot about ropes and knots. He professed to know a lot about many things. Cars and girls and electricity and raccoons were among the subjects he lectured me about. I always listened—whether I believed him or not—because he was Connor, the one who had befriended me when I fell into junior high school, no rope attached, no safety net, a small, skinny, awkward and friendless specimen of pre-adolescence.

I found out later, after the incident with the rope, that very few people liked Connor. He was an egomaniac, pushy and quick to dismiss the opinions of others. While I admired him for his air of authority, others saw that air as simply swagger. I had felt flattered that he had chosen me above all the interesting, smart, athletic boys in our class, but the pool he was able to choose from didn't contain any of those people. It contained me. There might have been a few other losers treading water along with me in that murky pool. For whatever reason, I was the one his net dragged in.

It's an old story, and there's no need to go into it. I will say that I gained a great deal from our relationship. His information on girls was faulty. So was his information on raccoons, for that matter. But we kept each other company at a time when we both might have been alone.

We lived in a small town on a medium-sized river. The town had seen better days and worse ones. It was not big enough for skyscrapers, but it thought a lot of itself like many small towns. Its people were the people of America, largely middle-class and unexceptional. But it had once boasted a well-to-do family who lived in a stately house on a small hill by the medium-sized river. By the time of my childhood, the family had been mostly forgotten. Years later I found a local history that enlightened me. The family name was Johnson. The patriarch was a go-getter. He tinkered with this and that in the nineteenth-century style, but just before the Civil War, he constructed a steam-powered rolling mill. It made him rich, his wealth stacked high like the bodies at Gettysburg. He built his house in 1875. It had three floors and many rooms and held him and his wife and eight children along with a plethora of servants. He died in 1890, and his progeny scattered to the four winds. The house sat empty until 1912 when it burned.

After the fire and a near century of neglect, the foundations could still be seen, crumbling and moss-covered, peering from weedy patches of undergrowth. One other feature of the estate survived. At the edge of the property on a bluff above the river were two large, sheet-metal tubes that ran from the cliff edge down to the river seventy-five feet below. These tubes were garbage chutes, the way the Johnson family disposed of its waste. It was a different time, so it never occurred to them that throwing garbage into a river was a bad practice. That's what rivers were for.

There were two tubes, each about two feet in diameter. Their tops extended about a yard above the ground. They had been covered with hinged lids, whether originally or later I do not know. On my first visit to the spot with my father, the hinges still worked creakily. Later a fence was put around the property, and the lids were fastened down with screws or welds; I don't remember exactly. The fence was probably scaled before it had even been finished. The lids lasted a little longer, but by the time Connor and I visited, they had not only been torn open, but had disappeared, leaving the tubes like two gaping mouths waiting hungrily for garbage.

Which they received, of course. Candy wrappers and napkins and cigarette butts were supplemented by rocks and pebbles and twigs and branches. No doubt the occasional hat or glove joined the mix, stolen from unfortunate boys not unlike myself. It's odd to make the comparison, but this debris hardly measures up to the nineteenth-century deposits: the kitchen offal, the night soil, the ashes from the many fireplaces.

When Connor told me his plan, I was speechless with admiration. So many children, and adults for that matter, had stared into that darkness, wondering. But it was Connor who would take the next step.

It was a cold winter day between Thanksgiving and Christmas when we slogged to our destination. People referred to the estate as being in the town, but it was really several miles away down a dirt road, and we knew it was unlikely we would have any witnesses. We went through one of the many holes in the aging fence. Atop the hill we had a view of the brownish river. At this distance it seemed as still as a pond. Across the river lay a few more hills, also dressed in wintertime brown. This year's fallen leaves lay deep around their trunks, but all we could see were the bare branches and some rocky outcrops and the occasional green splash of a pine tree.

We crossed the hilltop, skirting the old foundations. I carried Connor's flashlight. He himself had a coil of rope over his shoulder. The rope was a pleasant tan color and unfrayed. It looked new and expensive. Connor told me he had stolen it from a boat docked on the river.

Everything he owned had been acquired in some exploit, some feat of derring-do. As he regaled me with his latest tale, I listened docilely.

I had no idea how to descend into the depths of a garbage chute. Ropes and knots and climbing might as well have been postgraduate math for me. Connor was unfazed by the challenge. He affixed the rope to a nearby tree. "That's a half-hitch knot," he told me. "It's what sailors use. That knot can hold an ocean liner."

I nodded agreeably as he wrapped two turns of the rope around his waist. "See, you wrap around twice. Then it'll hold. That's how they climb Mount Everest." He looked at the rope approvingly. "Give me the flashlight."

I handed him the flashlight.

"See, you just let it out a little at a time," he said. He gave the rope a yank, testing the ocean liner knot.

I peered over the edge into the blackness. "Connor," I ventured. "How will you get back up?"

He was momentarily speechless, a rarity. "I just pull myself up," he answered, recovering quickly. "With the rope. The same way I go down."

That reassured me. I had trouble envisioning the process, and I knew I wouldn't be able to do it. But Connor knew things.

We had no idea what Connor would find. The bottoms of the tubes had been plugged up for decades, whether deliberately or not I had no idea. That he would only find sticks and pebbles and candy wrappers was inconceivable. Something had to be in that lurking darkness. Something sinister or the solution to an unknown mystery or a fortune in stolen money. Something.

"Okay." Connor hauled himself onto the edge of the tube. He adjusted the rope around his waist. He pulled the rope taut. "Now we'll..." he began as he swung free of the tube's edge. The rope took his full weight. But Connor didn't really know about knots. The half-hitch unraveled.

The knot ceased to be a knot and became simply rope, and it trailed just behind Connor as he disappeared into the blackness. As far as I could tell, he didn't scream.

I knew what I'd seen, but I couldn't believe it. I stood stock still. My vision clouded, then a sort of picture frame surrounded what I saw in front of me, and the picture itself darkened, then throbbed rhythmically. I felt unsteady. I grabbed the edge of the tube to support myself, but as I touched it I felt such revulsion that I let it go. My knees wobbled, so I sat on the cold ground. A light wind disturbed the sparse grass around me.

Gradually the shakiness left me. My vision became normal, and I carefully stood up. I was afraid to look down the tube. I turned to the tree where the half-hitch knot had failed so suddenly. I studied the trunk to make sure there was no rope attached to it. Just in case the disaster had sprung from my imagination. I glanced up at the sky. The light-gray clouds shifted and swirled, and I wasn't sure if they were being battered by the wind or if this was another trick of my vision. It made me dizzy all over again, and I lowered my eyes. When the dizziness passed, I turned and walked away, back across the former lawn of the Johnson estate, skirting the old foundations, through the hole in the fence and home.

There must have been quite a turmoil at Connor's house in the next few days. Anxiety, tears, anger, resentment, grief. Parents and relatives and police and teachers. It must have been agonizing.

I was known to be Connor's friend, so of course they came to me with questions that they posed in gentle and reassuring voices.

My parents watched me secretly, looking for signs of trauma, expecting loss to break out on me like poison ivy. I appeared obstinately normal. And in fact, I was normal. My life had changed. Connor had helped me in so many ways, and now I had to approach the world differently. At this I was only middling successful. But I never felt grief or any sense of loss. As young and tender as I was, I should have staggered under the weight of this death. It should have pained me, left me desolate. But I passed through it as if I had studied Eastern mysticism, as if I believed that death is but an illusion, as if I heard the sound of one hand clapping.

I can't explain that. I have suffered other deaths since, and they have left me weak and bereft, my mourning broken only by occasional flashes of anger. I also can't explain why I never revealed what happened. I told them I hadn't seen Connor that Saturday, that I had no idea where he might have gone, though he had said something about the river. By Christmas the frantic searches had exhausted the possibilities, and it was generally assumed that Connor had drowned, that the river had swallowed him up as it used to swallow up the garbage of the Johnson estate.

Psychologists and other students of the human mind would have their theories about my silence. Maybe one of them is right. Maybe all of them. The one theory I would like to lay to rest is that I was scared. I was not scared that I would be blamed or be talked about or be ostracized. I don't mean to say that I was brave. I just mean that these possibilities never occurred to me.

I go back up the hill now and then. To the old Johnson estate. The place is still fenced off, but decades of trespassers have rendered the fence useless and impotent, and much of its wire mesh has been trampled to the ground, where weeds conceal it as they do the foundations of the once-elegant house.

I don't go back as a memorial or ritual. I don't visit every year on the anniversary of the event and say a silent prayer for my friend. Nothing so dramatic. I just go to stroll and watch the river and look at the hillsides opposite. They are sometimes green and sometimes bare, as they were that day. Every year the subdivisions push a little farther up their sides.

So I stroll. I reminisce. Occasionally I will see children dropping rocks down the garbage chutes, waiting expectantly for them to hit the bottom.

—WILLIAM BRASSE (he/him)

A dry, dusty smell hits Randolph when he opens the doors. The smell twists his stomach and he feels every muscle in his body tense. He takes a deep breath and pushes through it, stepping in but keeping his head down to avoid all the eyes.

"Randy!" A plump, white woman wearing a floor length black dress scurries up the aisle towards him.

"Hi, mom," Randolph says. He looks up to see her and his mind immediately registers the dozens of stained glass images along the clerestory. The images he once considered his friends, both a comfort and an escape, now stare at him, crowding him. He smiles weakly and gives his mom a brief hug before shoving his hands into his pockets and bowing his head slightly to avoid the stares from the stained glass.

"You'll sit with me in the front row. If anyone asks, you couldn't make it to rehearsal and that's why you're not a pallbearer," his mom says.

"Sure," he nods slightly.

Not many people have arrived yet, thankfully. Randolph would like to be able to see his father, but the closed casket means otherwise, so instead he stays in his pew. His foot taps incessantly. He can't stop it. He needs a smoke. He desperately tries to keep his nerves down and relax his muscles, but his pulse is racing, and he's sweating through the suit jacket. He closes his eyes, does a few breathing exercises, and focuses his mind on his father's life, the only thing worth commemorating by putting up with this shit.

He had suggested an outdoor funeral at dad's favorite fishing dock, but his mom wouldn't hear of it. She had said the church was just too beautiful to waste, or something along those lines. Lots of her friends had hosted funerals there; this was her opportunity.

The church is beautiful, though, Randolph admits. It has cathedral-like stained-glass scenes from the *Bible* that allow the sun to illuminate the pews and large pipe organ. It had been a Catholic Church, but when their attendance numbers dwindled, the small community chose to merge with another nearby Catholic community for services. Now it is home to the First Baptist congregation, with the exception of the small Catholic cemetery to the right. The First Baptist church took the empty grounds to the left of the building that had been allotted for the expansion of the cemetery: a dream that was never realized by the previous congregation. In turn, First Baptist Church turned it into a private cemetery for church congregants, which had caused the congregation to experience significant growth, and now, that's where Randolph's father is to be buried, not next to Grandpa and Grandma in the old family plot.

Soon, people fill in the pews behind Randolph. He listens to the shuffle of feet and increasing chatter. His brothers had arrived just after him. His mom greeted them and positioned them to greet guests near the doors, but none of them had come to greet him. When everyone finally is seated—he next to his mom in the front and his three brothers with their families in the second row—Pastor Kent walks down the aisle to the right of the podium decorated by fake Easter lilies. Then, Randolph hears footsteps he would recognize anywhere. His gut drops and he finds himself holding back vomit.

He leans close to his mother and whispers, "What . . . what . . . Why is Parsons here?" His foot taps relentlessly. He needs a smoke.

His mom whispers back, "I know you and Pastor Parsons have had . . . issues, but he was a good friend of your father's!"

Randolph sits back. His foot tapping. His hand automatically moves to his breast pocket looking for his cigarettes. David Parsons steps behind the podium and looks around at the guests, sweeping his broad smile around the room and briefly making eye contact with Randolph. He begins to speak but Randolph doesn't hear anything. His mind plays back cursed tales of boys' nights hosted by Youth Pastor Parsons, sleeping bags in the sanctuary, being visited in the middle of the night, his mind wandering and pretending to be just a figure in the stained glass watching unspeakable seductions from the clerestory. He doesn't feel himself stand up. He doesn't feel himself grab his smoke pack, but when the cigarette touches his lips it brings him back into himself. He turns his head slowly. Everyone is staring. Head crouched, he rushes out the side door amidst whispers, and makes his way to the new cemetery, where a hole in the ground waits for his father.

It's not like the people here don't know what happened. The trial was in the paper for weeks, but when Randolph lost, the congregation welcomed Parsons back with open arms. He never would have come back to this damned place if it weren't for his father.

Tears fill his eyes as his shaking hands finally light a much needed cigarette. "Hey, Dad," he says, taking a drag and sinking down into the dirt next to an empty grave, "I— I— I miss you. I wanted to uh, take you fishing one last time, but I— I guess that wasn't in the cards for us." He takes another pull and feels his body relax just a little bit. His father had always accepted him, and just been good to him in general. He didn't know how to take the news about what had happened, and he never openly said anything about Parsons outright, but Randolph had noticed a change in him. His father didn't talk to Parsons after everything came out: two years of silence before, during, and for the brief period after the trial but before his death. It's disgraceful to have that man lead the funeral.

Randolph puts his cigarette stub out on the overturned dirt. Maybe he should leave. He thought after all this time he could get through being in the sanctuary, but seeing Pastor Parsons was another thing entirely. Now, after running out of the funeral, would he even be accepted at the graveside? Randolph hears the creaky cemetery gate swing open, unexpected. It's too soon for the service to be over. He looks up. A tall blonde man, wearing a wool trench coat over a light blue button up shirt and black slacks, walks through the gate.

"Tony!" Randolph shouts. Tony looks at him and smiles, closing the gate behind him. He strolls confidently towards Randolph.

Randolph stands up and says, "But this is a two hour drive for you!" He wipes tears from his eyes.

Tony embraces him, kisses him, and says, "I know we haven't been seeing each other that long, but I woke up and realized I couldn't let you do this day by yourself, so I looked up the only Baptist cathedral in the state and hoped it was the right one."

"I can't believe you came! I was just thinking about leaving. My mom . . . Parsons is doing the ceremony—" Tears flood Randolph's eyes again as he shakes and Tony wraps him in a big hug.

"If you want to leave, I can drive you home. I got a rental just in case," he says.

"What! That— that is so sweet. What did I do to deserve you?"

"I know; I'm pretty great," Tony says and gives Randolph a wink.

Randolph lets out a congested chuckle, then wipes his eyes and nose. He takes in a deep breath and lets it out slowly, then says, "Thank you. I definitely want to ride back together. I thought I wanted to leave, but with you here, maybe we can stay?" He looks at Tony, gives him a hopeful smile, and adds, "Besides, can you imagine the look on Mom's face?"

"I definitely wasn't expecting to meet her like this, but I feel like it's kind of perfect."

Randolph gives a short haggard laugh, "It really is."

The two stand together at the grave, talking about Randolph's father. Tony's arm is wrapped around him as he oscillates between tears and laughter. After another thirty minutes or so, the doors open and Randolph's brothers and uncle carry out the coffin. Several people begin whispering once they notice the gay couple at the graveside. Randolph's youngest brother frowns heavily, and his mother gasps audibly from across the cemetery. Already positioned, there is nowhere for his family to stand but next to them as they lay Randolph Senior to rest.

—DIXIE/DAMON KOOTZ-EADES (it/its)

black holes

There it is again—the urgent scratching of hoof or tooth against wood.

There's a hatch leading to a cellar next to the outside wall. The deer is trying to make you look. Time you dragged yourself out of bed to see what she wants.

This whole thing won't stop until you do.

You were in a peaceful sleep—the most restful for a long time, because this old Hebridean island chapel is dark-dark, and quiet as a mouse-house. Although you know it's silly, you're worried about things that thrive in the black, like ghosties—the ones who say, "You don't belong here, lassie." No, you're a city girl, and not even a girl, actually, nor a boy. *What are you?* This question bothers you. It's why you came here, to write an answer. Otherwise known as: *a story.*

The story was sitting in your head, clearer than ever, before you went to sleep. Now the deer noise has made it difficult to grasp and so frustratingly pre-conceptual.

Exasperated, you throw off the covers and place your feet on the stone floor. Freezing, although the air has less of a chill because the log fire has been burning all day. The deer is getting frantic, louder still. You walk to the door, which is heavy, arched, and with a big old key that clunks in the lock as you turn it. When you step out, you see stars—audaciously rich clusters of stellar bodies who surprise you every time.

It's too cold for just pyjamas so you step back in and grab an old coat and woollen socks from the hooks beside the door which are always full of outdoorsy things. You also pull on a pair of too-big wellies, then you walk-shuffle to the cellar hatch intending just to scare the deer. You're nearly next to her by the time she looks at you—dead in the eye—like *you're* the animal.

After holding for a moment, the deer springs into the hills at the back of the chapel. You take a closer look at the hatch. There's a mark. A circle with a ten-point star inside. You look up and see an ultra-bright star directly above you—closer than you've ever seen and it's getting closer. Up, you keep looking. Towards the ground-star the deer found, you scuffle. Up, down, up down—until you're standing directly on the hatch-star and looking up at the sky star—then you are:

Gone, straight up.

***

There's a glint between the rocks in the bay—the bay you can see from the chapel—just near where the sea is lapping. From there, you can also see a clear view of the distillery.

You went there for a walk one evening—in fact, you've done that at about the same time, every evening, of the ten you've been staying on the island.

"But I was gone last night, and I arrived back again by the morning, and I'm going for a walk, again." you say, just before you head out.

"I'm in a loop?" you say as you close the door.

Not telling.

What was that?

Nothing.

One foot in front of the other as bloody usual, feeling like you don't fit. That's okay. In fact, that's good.

Back to the shiny thing. It's a battery, from what you can see—one of those small flat ones that go in watches and the like. Pick it up quickly before it gets too dark to see.

"I love you," shouts a voice that seems to be coming from the small shed surrounded by old buoys, ropes, and lobster pots, with no light inside or out. You look around for the owner of the voice.

"Where are you?" you shout. "I can't see you."

"Oh, sure you can't. You know very well where I am," *someone* shouts back.

"Damn well don't," you mutter to yourself, as you bend down to pick up the battery. You pocket it. This would never happen in London, you think.

"Try looking in their eye, then," the voice says, quieter than before.

***

Right, let's get this straight. Although not *too* straight.

Do you remember when there was another day when you went for a morning walk—as well as an evening walk—the first time after the deer-hatch, you think.

As you were approaching the distillery on the other side of the bay, a big ginger dog bounded out of one of the fisherman's cottages. There was no one accompanying her. Or him. Them. The dog circled you twice and then sat in front of you, like a good boi. Boi is gender neutral.

The dog said, "Yes that's right. Now all you need to do is find the passage, which will lead you to the story. I think you're stuck on the idea that it goes up because you know you'll end up in heaven one day. But that's not where heaven is, actually."

"Where is it then?" you asked.

The dog seemed to refuse to answer and just sat there blinking in the silence. You were aware of how shiny the dog's nose was. Such big eyes, too.

"There's no need to stare," said the dog. You took a step closer so you could stroke the dog's head and take a proper look at the dog's pupils which were the darkest and biggest you had ever seen. Looking at them felt like being drawn into a hug from death, actually. Or a womb.

Suddenly there was a loud bleat from a sheep—do you remember? You looked out over the hills of the hinterland and thought about how lucky you were to be there. The sheep was persistent. The dog was still sitting. You chose the sheep.

"Fine. It's so hard to get you people to listen," said the dog as they walked away.

The dog left behind a toy—a child's toy car. Or yours. Green. You pocketed it, once the sheep stopped holding your attention.

***

"Nonbinary doesn't really cover it." I've heard you say that often through how you move.

The beaches on the island look like the moon.

That was where you went after picking up the green toy car. Little did you know that when you were walking on that beach, you actually *were* walking on the moon. It was just that you weren't there, if that makes sense.

You marvelled at sea vegetables sprawled across the sand and you noted how you didn't know the gender of any of them. Behind you were several cows, since the fields dissolve into the sand which becomes the sea, that's the way life is.

"I need to write all this stuff down. I need to document my time on this island. And publish it, with the most prestigious press I can. Before I forget it. Or die, and everyone forgets *me*," you said to the sky. A tear made its way down your cheek.

I wouldn't worry about that if I were you, which I am.

The story is already here—it's already out in the world—even in its incoherent, disordered beauty—since *I* can see you, my grief turned grace. *The great reader in the sky, me.*

Anyway, so, then you walked towards the sea, being careful not to stand on the greenery. How wonderful the sky looked, aflame—the sun was beginning to sink at the end of another short Hebridean winter day. The waves were choppy and hostile—and when you noticed that—this was when you remembered the car in one pocket and the battery in the other. You took them out and held one in each hand.

Your logical writing head threw up unhelpful thoughts like what if you can't unscrew the battery compartment since you don't have the correct tool? Luckily, the cover was missing so it was possible to just press the battery in. In it clicked. Did you like the sound?

What if you were to paddle in the freezing sea? I thought how refreshing it would be—like ice to a wound—although I also knew you wouldn't believe me.

OK, instead, I thought, what if you encountered a fairy—right there—by the oddly shaped trees that straddle the farmland and the moon-beach? You seemed much more up for this, which made me happy.

"Fairy? Are you there?" you said, feet rooted in the lunar sand and sea crashing behind you. Bluster was growing in the air. I didn't say there *would* be a fairy;, I said 'what *if?*'

"Yes of course I am." Okay, fine, there you are then.

"Are you real?" you asked.

"What a stupid question," the fairy answered. It *was* a stupid question.

"What gender are you?" you asked.

"And another one. You can't go around asking stuff like that. If god herself was here with us, would you ask her the same? Would you ask the island? Would you ask a *heart?*" The fairy emerged out of the shadows, slowly stretching a long, scrawny, green leg into the light, followed by a body just as thin. Lustrous locks and a pretty goblin face.

"That's just one of the things we humans have to ask. We need the knowledge., you reply, in the middle of your judgments, perhaps feeling somewhat ashamed.

"Just make sure you don't say things about knowledge-*smowledge* when you see *you know what,*" said the fairy, looking sexy.

"*What?*" you asked, blush creeping up your neck. Yes, the fairy was gorgeous, and cheeky, I know. That's why I decided you should meet—your story deserves joyous spice.

"Oh, darling, that's right—I'm all meat—no fur, no fear. Just go ahead and *eat,*" said the fairy. How *devastating.* "All those unnecessary accoutrements, all that seeing and recognition, those are the issues. Not the flesh itself."

"I can't understand you. You don't exist anyway," you said.

"Oh, oh. For sure. Now you're getting it. Nor do you, outside of 101010, Mx nonbinary." The fairy disappeared, not at all heartbroken.

You then turned your attention to the little car and switched it on. It sang, *how much is that doggy in the window?*

***

I'll go back to the dog, you thought, *because that seemed to be what the car was suggesting.*

"Non-existence is existence!" you shouted at the sky. I guess that was your try at a neat soundbite, or having some power in the face of your perceived weakness.

Nice try, but not quite, I whispered.

Before looking for the dog, you cooked dinner. Locally caught scallops sautéed in butter with lemon and cracked pepper, samphire on the side. A small dressed crab to start. How thick the anticipation, how I was glad to see you give yourself deep love by eating deliciously with yourself. It would have been perfect if you'd then masturbated and had a hot bath, but of course instead the shell of the dressed crab asked you to shrink and carry it on your back.

"Don't talk shit," you said, out loud. You got up—in a slight huff—to do the washing-up while looking out of the tall window into the trees behind the chapel. The hot water was a balm upon the disappointment of being unable to squeeze into the crab shell. That was when you heard the barking outside. You considered whether you'd heard it before on previous nights and it occurred to you that yes, actually, you had.

You took out the car again and without thinking, walked to the bay and repeatedly played the tune, *how much is that doggy in the window*, until you eventually became so tired you could barely stand.

***

When you returned to the chapel, ready for sleep, the dog from the fisherman's cottages was sitting in a perfect doggy pose, just outside the door. You had ghosty-fear again.

"You're right, my friend," said the dog.

"I am? Should I scream?" you asked.

"Aye, you probably should. Your mind is about to be blown," said the dog, lifting a paw and cocking its head to one side.

"How so?" you asked.

"D-O-G backwards is what, my friend?" said the dog.

"You're *god*?" you asked.

"Don't be ridiculous. But wouldn't it be wonderful if I were?" said the dog. "I am, however, a good friend of hers. Like that fairy that lives on the lunar beach, except I'm way better than them—I have even less genders."

"Is that good?" you asked, fishing the key from your pocket.

127

"*Good* question," said the dog. "Why don't you take a closer look into my eye."

You did just as the dog asked. You knelt to meet the dog's eye—closer, closer still—until there was nothing but black.

That's when you felt a rolling in your chest—like having a septum piercing—and then a kick-back from a gun, and when you awakened, you were inside sleep. Not in a dream, but in a black velvet capsule.

***

So here we are.

It feels soft, smells of aniseed, and other dark things like chocolate, coffee, any other dark medicine—wool, oil, smoke, charred meat from a BBQ, plum pudding, black vanilla, poppy seed and all the deliciousness of anything that isn't light. Arousal and bad romance, kink and naughty jokes. Gay sex, oh so much gay sex. Peaty soil of Hebridean islands. Drinking bodily fluids. Eating, indulgence. Black pudding and black sheep. Being an outsider, forest spirit dwellers, black-out cake, and liquid love. Oh yes, this *should* be hell, by most accounts—but it isn't. Do you know what it is?

"No, I don't," you say.

"Yes you do." I reply—*can you hear me now? Can I give up on the speech marks?*

"Yes, but you're muffled," you say.

"Fine, I'll keep them for now. Keep moving around, it feels good, for me. Dance about, cover yourself in my insides, my precious one." I say.

"Who does it feel good for?" you ask.

For me.

"Who's me?"

Me.

...

You're inside me. A black hole, my friend; some call me a singularity, some call me a collapsed star. Collapsed star-quality, that's me—*slay.*

"I can barely hear you. Am I dead?"

"Sorry. I'll return to the old human formalities, again. Who could say whether you've met death, or not? There's so many of them."

"I would have thought *you* could," you say.

"Fair. But then, you did come to me through my good friend dog."

"Jesus Christ."

Still wrong.

"I *am* in heaven, aren't I?" you ask.

"Black hole. One of my vagina-multiples. As I said. It's more like you're inside my body of work, so that's bloody close. Fairly rude, really, that you earth lot tend to call me a black hole—suggests some kind of endless darkness. But that's accurate, I suppose. Your story should note that darkness isn't bad. Instead, it's a big genderless playground."

"What's that sound?" you ask.

"Oh, I guess the auditory side of things is a little more challenging inside here. Echoes are a problem since this is where sounds come to rest. You're probably hearing that wretched dog song. He thinks it's funny. It's time you realised something. You'd better go back."

"What? How do I end this? The mystery is still here," you say. *Now you're getting it.*

"What was that last bit? *Hello?* Put the punctuation back," you say, before I send you back to the chapel. Pray. Have a cuppa and a piece of shortbread. Whisky if you like it—I can't stand the stuff.

***

I'm not surprised you've gone to bed. You sleep as soon as your head hits the pillow.

The trouble is that it's not even been an hour and there's that scratching again.

Here we go again. Up you get, tired, feeling inadequate about your gender—maybe an affirming haircut will do it—and then out, with the coat and socks from beside the door, outside and fearing the ghosties, and then to the hatch. You scare the deer—or rather the deer just knows that it's

129

time for it to go to where it needs to in the story. The bright star, the circle, looking up and into the sky.

This time, you manage to cling to consciousness and not be thrown into the next day.

You don't sleep, and instead, you look *me* in the eye. And you don't end up in one of my many vaginas, nor on my skin on the lunar beach with my toy. I suppose the least I can do is address you with the truth. The end for your story, and the beginning, and the middle—and all those things like structure, voice, point of view and cadence.

I'll give you something to live with and by and through.

You are frightened-deer-D-O-G-cosmos loop with scrumptious food-no crab shell-walking-mind-fuck-intermission-in my image.

You are holy.

Get inside my metaphysical.

—VIC BROOKS (they/them)

Previously published in NonBinary Review

The house on Buena Avenue had been fashionable once but had fallen into disrepair between its construction and when James Laurent acquired the property. He was moderately successful doing business as a spiritual guide and medium. "Moderately successful" meaning M. Laurent made ends meet due to a short list of wealthy, elderly women clients, from whom he was able to wring enough to cover his basic needs. New customers to the Buena Avenue house were virtually nonexistent. Thus, it was of great surprise to him when the bell rang in the middle of dinner on an evening in August.

M. Laurent peeped out from a window overlooking the wide porch and saw a young man, rather awkwardly dressed in a too-big gray suit, waiting at the front door. He watched the younger man for several minutes wondering. The young man shifted his weight back and forth and ultimately rang again. Laurent's surmise that this boy was soliciting gave him pause, but he finally answered the door when it seemed that the visitor was not going away. As the door opened, Laurent saw the youth's stone face transform into a wide smile and a right hand reach toward him, "Mr. Laurent? How good to meet you!" the smiling young man exclaimed. Laurent falteringly held out his own hand to be taken in a forceful handshake. The two men stood there shaking hands for a moment, and finally, the visitor cautiously said, "May I come in? I'd like to take up a moment of your time. I know you must be very busy!" Laurent smirked and moved aside for the boy to enter.

"Well, you seem to know who I am, young man," Laurent said with condescension, even though he was a bit flattered. "Now why don't you tell me who you are and what has brought you to my home in the middle of the dinner hour?" He ushered the visitor into his reception room.

"Pardon me, sir," the boy replied, ignoring Laurent's conceit of going by *monsieur*. "I'm a great admirer. My name is McSwain, Michael McSwain."

"Do have a seat, Mr. McSwain," Laurent indicated a chair. "You requested a moment of my time, so I assume you have something to sell?"

"Like I said," the boy gulped, "I am a great admirer of your work. I've heard of you from Mrs. Gately, and I wanted to . . . er . . . well, sir, I wanted to approach you with a proposal to act as your assistant, or apprentice you might say." Laurent looked blankly at the youth. Whatever would give him the idea? How was he acquainted with the Gately widow, to whom Laurent ministered once a week. He'd never seen the young man around her Lincoln Park mansion. Laurent appraised McSwain again. He couldn't be more than 25 years old; dark hair; a square jaw; handsome, in a rather working-class kind of way. Finally, Laurent replied coolly, "I had never considered having an apprentice, and I don't really think I have need of one. You see, mediumship is a gift; it's not a skill you pick up at a trade school."

"Sir, I completely understand, and I didn't mean to imply anything of the sort," McSwain said, recovering quickly from the rebuke in Laurent's voice. "You see my mother was a bit gifted herself, and did card readings for Mrs. Gately. That's how I came to know her," he explained.

"Mr. McSwain," Laurent replied, relishing the higher ground he felt he inhabited, "cartomancy and table rapping, trumpets and spirit boards are parlor tricks. Mediumship is a delicate relationship between a human being and the spiritual world. It is a dance; it is intimate; the spirits I bring up for my clients inhabit my body and use me as their *nuntius.*"

"How can you know I don't—or my mother, for that matter—have this gift?" McSwain said rather defiantly, dropping the previous obsequiousness, "Look here, Laurent, Mrs. Gately has mentioned that you are barely making ends meet. Your grand house here is in disrepair, and hardly welcoming to new customers. I think I can help you upgrade your image, so to speak, and perhaps hone my own—*gifts* as part of the bargain." McSwain warmed to his argument, "I'm not asking for any money, just take me on, give me a place to stay. I'll do any menial tasks you wish; just help me learn!"

Laurent sat back in his chair and pressed his fingers together, making a steeple. He looked McSwain up and down again. A multiplicity of thoughts passed through his head. No exchange of money, and the boy was handsome. It wouldn't hurt to have a companion in the house. Maybe McSwain *could* help drum up business, with his good looks alone. Finally, Laurent leaned forward, "All right, Mr. McSwain," he said, "I'm willing to take the chance if you are. Come back in a few days with your things."

***

Michael McSwain returned on the appointed day, and M. Laurent took him up to a room on the third floor. It had been swept and dusted and contained a bed, chair, chifforobe, and one circular window high on the wall. "If you stand on the chair and squint, you can see the lake from here,"

132

Laurent offered. "Once you're finished settling in, come down and we can discuss your duties."

"Thank you, sir," the young man replied, setting down his briefcase and small valise on the bed. "I'll be down in just a few minutes."

"Take your time," said Laurent, turning in the doorway, "I'll be in the spirit room—just off the reception room." Laurent closed the door and returned to the stairwell.

That evening, Laurent and McSwain settled in for a long discussion about the expectations for the apprenticeship. Laurent rattled off a list of menial tasks he'd like McSwain to complete on a regular basis, and McSwain responded with queries about avenues by which he could learn a bit about M. Laurent's gifts. Hesitatingly, Laurent agreed to let McSwain prepare the spirit room for appointments as well as attend sittings with select clients. After several hours of conversation and deal-making, the two men finally shook hands over the table in the spirit room, both feeling like their futures looked prosperous.

***

After several weeks of cleaning the house on Buena Avenue, preparing all the meals, organizing M. Laurent's abysmally kept office, and arranging client meetings, McSwain was finally allowed to observe a sitting. M. Laurent led McSwain through the preparations of the spirit room with exacting detail, then double-checked that everything was in place: the windows fastened, drapes entirely closed, two chairs placed opposite each other at the circular table, a stopped mantlepiece clock placed to the left of M. Laurent's chair, finally, another chair pressed against the dark green, acanthus leaf-patterned wallpaper.

At 5:00pm the bell rang. McSwain showed an elegant woman with a fur wrap and diamond brooch into the reception room. "Mrs. Haggarty," Laurent said, entering the room and taking her hands, "Let me introduce my new apprentice, Mr. McSwain. He will be assisting me with the sitting tonight." Mrs. Haggarty nodded, noticing, in afterthought, Michael's handsome face and well-made proportions. A smile fluttered and then she gave her attention back to the medium as he led her into the spirit room. McSwain took his seat as client and medium settled into their chairs at the damask-covered table.

133

"Mr. McSwain, if you would dim the lights, please," M. Laurent said solemnly, as they had rehearsed earlier that day. "Mrs. Haggarty, as you'll recall from our last sitting, once I am in trance and your daughter arrives, you'll have fifteen minutes at most to converse with her." Mrs. Haggarty nodded in a child-like way, belying her aged appearance. McSwain turned the lights down, impressed by the command his master had over the client. He'd heard old Mrs. Gately speak of the experience but wasn't quite ready for the power in Laurent's voice. The three of them sat in darkness for a few minutes. The atmosphere in the room became close. Mrs. Haggarty sat very straight, her eyes fixed on Laurent, whose head was bowed. After a few more minutes of silence, Laurent, reached out and set the hands of the mantlepiece clock to fifteen minutes past the hour. "Madame, the spirits draw near. Prepare yourself." Laurent continued with head bowed. A hum seemed to begin in the corner of the room and circle the three sitters, buzzing in one ear and then the next in a counterclockwise rotation.

"Mother?" Laurent's head rolled back on his neck. His eyes were filmy blue-white. The voice coming out of his throat was feminine, girlish.

"Oh yes, my darling!" Mrs. Haggarty leaned forward. "My darling, I'm here. I'm here again."

"Why do you disturb me. I am at peace," the voice seemed to emanate from Laurent's throat, but his lips did not move.

"Angeline . . . I," Mrs. Haggarty faltered, ". . . yes, I know. So you said the last time. I just needed to hear you one more time."

"Mother, the life you are living—the life I lived—is a temporary state. Afterwards spirits are in a beautiful abode of light. I know you are mourning my loss, but weep not for me."

"My dearest, I'm glad to hear it," the old woman said shakily, "Your happiness was all . . . is all I want. I just need you to tell me what happened. Why did you leave me?" McSwain could not take his eyes off of Laurent. How could this be real? He really had thought McSwain was a well-practiced charlatan. He'd come here to learn how to swindle stupid, old widows like Gately, whose credibility parted her from much of her inherited wealth.

"Mother!" Angeline/Laurent's voice hardened, "do not dig too deeply into the unknown!"

"Darling, was it something I did?" Mrs. Haggarty began to weep, "Did I fail you? You're speaking to me like I'm a stranger! Don't be angry with me, please." The old woman's voice became a pitiful squeak.

"Remove yourself from here. Leave me in peace," the voice snapped. "Yes, I took my life. I escaped the prison of my body." The hum in the room grew louder, enveloping the sitters, covering them like an uncomfortable blanket. Mrs. Haggarty continued to weep.

"Angeline . . ."

"OUT!" the voice screamed. Laurent's throat bulged. The table rattled. The hands of the clock clicked to the 12 on its face, and the humming abruptly lifted. The lights brightened, as if on cue. Mrs. Haggarty continued to weep, clutching at her fur as if it were a life preserver and she on the open sea. When Laurent emerged from the trance, his eyes back to brown from sickly white, he comforted the weeping woman at the table. McSwain sat half-stunned, half calculating.

***

A week after Mrs. Haggarty's sitting, the bell at the house on Buena Avenue rang again. McSwain answered the door to find a young woman, smartly dressed, her eyes veiled by dark glasses and her hair covered in a black and white scarf. McSwain led her into the reception room and alerted M. Laurent to her presence. The medium came in, surprised by a walk-in client. He deployed his most chivalrous greeting to the young woman. The woman removed her sunglasses and scarf, revealing a great beauty with sad eyes. She identified herself as Evelyn Lovegood, a resident of Evanston. She related to M. Laurent the recent loss of a dearly beloved uncle. Could the great medium help contact the spirit? The family seemed to be unable to locate a will. They were in such strife because of it. "Poor child," Laurent cooed. "Of course."

Laurent directed McSwain to hurriedly prepare the spirit room. The lights dimmed and the sitters in place, almost a reenactment of the sitting from seven days before, but for the youth and beauty of the client. "Now, my dear," Laurent began, "since this is your first sitting with me, what is the name of the spirit you'd like to contact. What was your dear uncle's name, so I can find him."

"Lefty . . . er . . . excuse me. Charles Lovegood," the young woman blushed at having accidently given a nickname.

135

"Excellent. Now . . . uh . . . Miss Lovegood, once your uncle makes his presence known, you'll have exactly fifteen minutes to speak with him. A medium's corporeal form can handle inhabitation by a spirit, not a minute longer," Laurent explained. He then added archly, "Of course we can make future appointments. Rest assured." Laurent bowed his head. Silence again until the hum returned to the room. McSwain gave Evelyn a reassuring look, unnoticed by Laurent. The medium reached out and set the clock hands to 12:15.

"Evelyn?" a deep voice arose from the blank, white stare of Laurent's upturned face. The young woman looked startled. The humming descended like a shroud again.

"I told you this guy's the real thing," McSwain said from the wall.

"Lefty . . . yes, it's Evelyn," she hesitated, "how are you, honey?" Laurent's body lurched in the chair.

"Evelyn," the voice seemed settled in. "Well look at you. And who's this?" Laurent's head snapped to the left, fixing its milky eyes on McSwain. "Well, well, well, together again, ain't we?"

"Look here, Lefty," interjected McSwain, "don't get sore. We didn't rat you out!"

"Oh, no?" the voice sneered, "then how's it that I'm here and you're out there?" Evelyn began to shake.

"Michael . . ."

"Can it, Evelyn," Lefty said from Laurent's throat. "You all ratted me out and I got the chair and now you call me up from . . ." Lefty blinked Laurent's eyes slowly. "What's this new con you got going?" McSwain got up and faced his former friend.

"It's a change of plans, we found a real-deal spirit man," McSwain shouted, "That money's not doing you any good in hell, so tell us where you stashed it!"

"Fuck you." Laurent's mouth said, the lips moving this time. Evelyn fainted. McSwain took Lefty by his borrowed body's lapels. A guttural laugh emerged from Laurent's slack lips. His throat started to expand. The mantlepiece clock hands ticked backwards toward the 12. McSwain released his right hand and pushed the hands back to 12:15. "Tell me now, you son of a bitch!"

"Ahh—" Lefty's voice sighed laughingly, descending further into a demonic bass, "Time's up, lover boy!" The uncomfortable hum in the room reached a crescendo. Lefty's voice rose. The room shook. Laurent's body jolted out of the chair and an eruption of gore spurted from his mouth.

***

The police arrived to check on a report of "some kind of explosion" on Buena Avenue. They entered the spirit room finding it decorated, as if for a birthday party, with James Laurent's entrails. The only recognizable bits of him left were his legs. A catatonic Evelyn was taken to Dunning Asylum. McSwain was taken into custody and questioned, but the young man never spoke again.

—LOUIS ALETANDO (he/him)

The two of us were talking for the first time in years when we expulsated. We began to ripple, as though two stones had been thrown into a pair of puddles shaped like bodies.

"I feel like I don't know what to say," and, "Yeah, me too," we were saying to one another, our voices still almost indistinguishable despite that we'd lived across the country from one another all this time.

And then we began to fold and twist, like taffy being pulled over a machine. The twists of us ballooned to fill the living room, spiraling, before finally coalescing into something like jellyfish chandeliers.

"Oh God . . ." and, "Oh God!" we whispered and shouted as we reached for each other, animated blown glass sculptures reenacting Adam and God from the ceiling of the Sistine Chapel. The both of us floated there above the couch in the otherwise unremarkable living room, the furniture dully mismatched, translucent, luminescent frills undulating until they touched with a sensation like sound. And then our worlds shattered into a thousand puzzle piece shards, visions of other realities.

***

Two women with our face stood below a vast skylight in the center of a ballroom bordered by dim arcades of red marble columns. The first woman, who wore a flower-patterned blue suit that made her look like a cross between a porcelain figurine and a sci-fi video game protagonist, stood braced as though against some great force. Her hands rippled and the whole of her gleamed as though she was becoming glass.

"Sister, please," said the second woman. She wore a vast dress of phthalo green ruffles, and the hand she placed on the first woman's shoulder was silver-skinned. "You must stop this experiment! You're—you're expulsating!"

***

The expulsations we'd become recoiled. Our heads reemerged first from the molten flows and then our hands, reaching for one another, though even at the airport we hadn't touched.

"Please," and, "You have to get ahold of yourself," we said to one another.

"Ahold of myself? You were always so—"

138

"Sorry, I didn't mean, just—"

***

An expulsation hunted a teenager under a green sky into a school gymnasium. His face looked like ours had at that age, but for his pink skin and baby blue hair. Other teenagers playing volleyball ran screaming when they saw the expulsation, but it was too late for them. When the expulsation touched them, they too began to expulsate, becoming a giant's toppled jewelbox of monstrosities, all chasing the boy. He leapt a fresh, slow moving expulsation, still getting its bearings and ran for the changing room.

"Help!" the boy shouted, banging on the locked door. On the other side, a blue-haired, teenage boy who also had our face widened his eyes in fear, fumbling with the lock.

***

"Sorry, I don't want to argue," and, "I don't either," we said, as we coalesced back into human shape, seated not where we had been, but rather standing, panting as though we'd just returned from running a minefield.

"Do you even remember why—?" and then, "Why we stopped talking?"

A rippling began by our ears and then consumed us.

***

In another branch of reality where the universe had started two decades later, two children with our face prodded sea anemones at the aquarium. We still remembered the clingwrap feeling of the tentacles around our small fingers. Beyond the touching pool, jellyfish in a columnar tank drifted, ballooning moons in the dark. The children turned to find their mother, to show her, because she loved beautiful things.

"Hey, look, it's dad," one of the children said, tugging on the other's shoulder. Their parents began to argue. The children began to cry silently watching their parents fight, fat tears streaming down their small, expulsating faces.

***

"I don't remember why we stopped talking either," and, "Was it our parents? Was it something I said, you said? Are we just not compatible? It had to have been something," we said.

139

It was something, and we both remembered, but in the moment we knew without speaking it was better to not remember, because what it was didn't matter. Trying to remember, maybe then arguing over the details, that would make it matter.

***

There was nothing anybody could do to stop an expulsation once it began to consume.

In every other world we witnessed, a version of us had expulsated. In one world, not a single patch of the violet sky was without an expulsation. In a second world, expulsations undulated over the blue grass under the green sky. In a third world, a lonely expulsation drifted aimlessly about a gray wasteland.

And now in our own world, we were expulsating, uncertain whether we could stop ourselves, knowing soon we would become just another pair of interdimensional entities consuming all there was.

***

 "I just wish . . . I wish we'd done this sooner," and, "Do you think we can try again?" we said and asked.

"I always wanted a twin," said in unison from the hearts of the expulsations we had become, this the joke we'd always once made and just now remembered after forgiving the other for whatever petty thing had come between us.

We embraced, eyes dry though we felt like we should be crying, expecting the world would soon be ending and uncertain, whether we made it through this or not, if our relationship could survive to restart itself. We both began to expulsate. Flashing undulations clashed, shattering until everything extraneous had atomized into opalescent dust. The shapes of us twisted, turning and pulling, quickly at first and then slowly until once again even the rippling had ceased, leaving only the two of us there in the living room. We were just twins who hadn't seen one another in years, siblings hoping to restart.

—EDWARD DASCHLE (he/him)

My brother's hands move stiffly, but at a lumbering pace, towards my father's neck. This is, obviously, a re-visualization in slow motion. Your hands do not *lumber* when you are trying to strangle someone.

I pace up, stumble on the side of the bed, waddle, and stop. I allow myself three seconds each to look at both, mostly to confirm the veracity of this spectacle, simultaneously hoping I do not regret the deflection in case they decide to kill each other. The skin on my father's neck dangles. His frame shrinks as he arches backwards.

I shift my gaze to my brother. He claws his hands into turtles and squirms. My brother is stout and the position he holds feels unconvincing, almost funny. I want to let out a chuckle but I hold back. My mother is also there. But like most mothers, she is a side character, small and underwhelming in her presence. Is my brother going to strangle my father? Not today, it seems.

I must admit today was a departure from the routine drudgery of our weekly scuffles, which take place every Sunday, inviolable as clockwork. A week is just perfect to let the four of us remain affixed to this inertia, the vector field of which has locked us in for almost three years. I am tethered.

In the last three years, I have learned to arrange my timetable around our ritual. On Sundays, I do not go out. I tell my friends I want to set up some time to write for a weekly book critic gig for a local newspaper. No local newspaper has space for book columns, let alone the money to pay for it. But my friends understand nothing about my work and believe me. I am the youngest in my family, only 24 years old, but at around 6 pm every Sunday, when the tension of an imminent fight starts enveloping us like a cloak, I patiently wait for the explosion. Then, I follow it up with moderating an exercise in pacification, starting with my father, then my brother, and finally my mother. I do this every week, only because they listen to me even though I am the youngest in the family. I do this every week, even when they learn nothing and their distressing behaviors continue to quietly circle our blood atoms.

But our ritual lasts only a few hours, following which we relapse into nothingness for the rest of the week. Which is when my world revolves S.

S. A lovely man I have had the honor to be loved by, I tell myself every day.

S, unlike a lot of men, cries. He cries without inhibitions. Sometimes his cry is a sniffle, sometimes it is a ghoulish bawl. Whatever it is depends *not* on how harrowing he thinks his circumstances are, but how likely he thinks that *I* will be perturbed by them. S cries when I cry, to whatever degree he can. I meet him every Sunday, and he brings me a fresh pack of my favorite cigarettes, Marlboro Double Burst, that we smoke as I recount the latest updates from the family altercation. In a fresh turn of events, my dad has declared he will not participate in any ceremony in my brother's marriage, nor will he give him any money to carry those on his own. The girl my brother wants to marry is petite, the kind that is probably undernourished, but that has indoctrinated generations of South Asian parents into believing that a woman like that does not give birth or survive childbirth. My parents proclaim, without a shred of evidence, that she has some problem, a disease, the exact nature of which she is trying to conceal from us. Approximately six months earlier, my brother had invited a girl from a different caste to our house. My father had slammed his phone on the floor till it disintegrated into dreamy, filamentous wisps. S tells me he does not understand why people hurt themselves when they are angry with others.

S listens to me intently. He always has something to offer, but he is quiet. Instead, he worms me into an embrace. I love how cushiony and warm he is because I am slender and veiny and always, always cold. He then clasps harder and mumbles a cry, and the bottom of my spine twists into an angry knot. I loosen my hold on him. He pulls me back in.

I am at S's place that he has rented in NCR and where I spend most of my Sunday nights. I am sprawled on his bed. S is looping his legs from under my thighs, probing my cellulite with the length of his nails. At this moment, I am the dear life he hangs on to, so I sit still. Intimacy's shifting nature is conspicuous in the room, which is dimly lit with yellow light that dissolves all the room's flaws, like a patchwork deployed to lend a deceptive orderliness to the device. On many days it looks like a cheap hotel room trying too hard to mask its unpalatable design—like semen spots on the bedsheet, fissures in the walls, cigarette burns on the curtains.

I release myself from S's hold and this time, he does not stop me. I get up and glance at his bookshelf placed against the wall along his bedside, as I often do when I need some space between us, and notice that he has added a new book that begins with a *How To*. S is a business analyst at a corporate firm, and that's all I know about his work. He has tried to explain to me several times what he does, but I don't get it no matter how much he simplifies it for me, just like I haven't understood how to tie shoelaces yet, and someone else tying them feels like they performed some magic trick.

I have realized that S's reading choices are partly what he is—5'8," with a groomed beard, thick eyebrows, and fluffy arms that he more than occasionally likes to flex to show off an insignificant muscle bumping out. He wears black, blue, and grey trousers that graze his hips in a gentle, uncorrupted form to the office. He drinks alcohol almost every day and posts about it on Instagram. He earns well. He loves his family.

He knows how to hold a room and everyone in it.

I feel S looking at me as he hands me a bottle of my favorite beer that he stocks up when I am staying with him. I know what he thinks I am thinking: that he is a frivolous man for whom reading is a self-neutralizing endeavor that helps him comply with the dogmatic ideas of right and wrong. That his intellect is so inadequate that he believes that everything starts at the beginning and unwinds to an end. Words start to tumble out of his mouth and flurry into hubris, but I am in no mood to surrender to our regulated dance of exchanging words that will tire me more than they will tire him. The fear of falling short of conversation with me frightens S, I know, though he won't admit it. That I will assuredly unscramble his inadequacies without verbalizing them terrorizes S even more. So, he packs those silences with words, futile words, each one of which bounces right off me but I listen on because that's a very small price to pay for all that he does for me.

I gulp down the beer in four large swigs and the alcohol stirs something in me. I examine S, who is now talking to his roommate, and spot a flicker radiating from his eyes, the kind that announces itself when one recalls their power in this world. I watch his face curve into glee, and feel mine twitch with annoyance. I allow myself to drown in this feeling for a quick moment because I like it for the thrill that some people get from, say, the idea of war. As I examine the scoop of his nose and the squint in his eyes, entirely stunned by the full shape of his existence, he turns his head and smiles at me—the smile that brought me down to my knees seven years ago—and I dissolve into pulp in a quick act of rebalancing.

S performs coin tricks to make me laugh; he learns new tricks every single month without fail so that I am not bored easily. He cooks chicken curry for me—he minces the chicken, marinates it, singes it like a fantasy—much in incongruity with his upper-caste, Brahminism conduct. He plans our fancy vacations and bears all major expenses. He shaves my pubic hair as I lie on my back to feel the warm buzz of the razor slither all the way up to my soul. He asks me to stay before I can lift a muscle to leave. He smells me, he touches me—my oily hair, my choppy fingernails, my sweaty underarms. He lingers, and then, he stays.

I think the root of most women's misery is that the men they are with are not monsters, but something worse. I could WikiHow How to Kill a Monster. And *probably* get away with it.

***

Once upon a time, in a short story I read on the Internet three years ago, men were not allowed into the real world until they had proven they could survive the company of women without destroying them. Every baby boy, a few quick moments after slipping out of the mother, would be whisked away to a fortified compound buried beneath the outskirts of the city. It would be a real place—with concrete walls, rusted gates, floodlights that never turned off. Then, as long as it would be necessary, 20 years or 50, they were raised by men and women who had never known how it was to be broken. Many of them hollowed out like beams eaten through by termites, and their number dwindled over time. Which was how the world tilted back into balance, until a revolution tore everything down.

I learnt that there are never any endings, only iterative rituals of collapsing and reassembling.

Back in the room, S grabs me with definite urgency. I feel a small log of his erection plodding me before I tell him that I am getting my period. He looks me in the eye, his forehead crinkled with suspicion, and announces that my date isn't until next week—around the 15th of the month—and I almost palpitate at my stupidity. S keeps a track of my menstrual cycle, of course. I feel my heart throbbing on the roof of my mouth but I keep a straight face. I tell him that dates keep shifting (a fact), and that I am going through some work stress that likely meddled with the hormones (a lie).

By now, I know that he knows. S stores moments like these like knives in a study drawer. He will brandish this one at a time when he would think that I would least expect it, except that I would have been expecting it all the time. Eventually, his distrust will prickle my face like a thousand microneedles until I have been shorn by the magnitude of my lies to him. The assault of my lack of morality would rock me back into his orbit, and he would say that I have done all of this to myself, which would not be untrue. Then, he would touch me, not so lovingly, and I will feel the cold creep up to my fingers and then to my throat, which is when I will throw up the weight of my undoings. What I mean is that he will begin to disappear and I will gasp for air until he begins to reappear.

****

S and I grew up in a time defined by an acute paucity of spaces to do as much as hold hands in peace. After school, in afternoons plump with aloofness, we would meet in the back lane of our colony park dotted by the chaotic spread of abandoned cars, which meant we could steal a few touches without worrying about being persecuted. I loved how S's dark skin glistened against the sweat even before we could do anything. He was exactly three inches taller, so he would kneel and drag my face closer to him through a deliberate movement of his hands that would make his arm muscles ripple, a quick look at which would immediately course an electric current through me. There was no sloppiness or disgusting gyrating of bodies and mixing of fluids. S's vulgarity was balanced, almost innocent, and I admired that about him. His touch was tender and cottony, just like the rest of him, and I would let that lift me and take me some place that was neither too warm nor too cold.

Soon after we started dating, S would fake a stomachache to bunk his class to sit outside mine. I would sneak him notes folded into origami hearts. He would break into a classic Shahrukh song as I passed by his class corridor during lunch hour. I would stop in my tracks and laugh loudly at his silliness, proud of this shameless flair for the drama. He would stand outside the main gate of our school with a strawberry ice cream cone that he bought from the money he stole from his mother, waiting on me for several minutes as the cream dribbled down his fingers in the scorching summer heat. I would lick the cream right off his fingers.

Being with S felt like living inside a house with a fridge that turned itself full before it emptied. S was a lover and something about it broke me, but with a kind of unexpected relief that I never imagined experiencing. There was nothing else to want.

S's friends never shied away from admitting that I was with S because he put me at the center of his existence. I would say that's not a full lie.* S made me feel like I could amount to something, and I wanted, very badly, to amount to something. And he did everything he could to leave me secure in this knowledge. I had put my weak, wanting heart into him. S was my world at the end of the world.

* I could talk about my part but that would take this story to a place
where it's not meant to be.

***

On April 5 of 2022, we are getting ready for dinner at our common friend M's place. M is a successful businessman, in ways that businessmen are usually successful, and S's closest friend. It's his late birthday party at his four-storey house in South Delhi. S and I are trying to decide what I should wear to look the part of the girlfriend of the best friend of a successful businessman.

S holds the red dress I'd pulled out against me and shakes his head, his face subtly giving away the dislike he feels at my choice. He says the neck is too deep, the silhouette too tight, and that as thin as I am, I don't have the breasts or the behind for a dress like that. I am torn between how I should feel—angry (because he is not supposed to tell me what to wear), worried (because just saying something, anything might start a fight) or apathetic (because he is factually correct—bodycon dresses really do not suit my tender frame).

I pick out another dress.

S, meanwhile, pulls out a shirt from his wardrobe, a blue with faint white stripes, and walks toward the iron stand. He plugs in the iron and begins to smooth the fabric with the kind of care he is known to extend to people.

But we are running late and he needs to take a shower, so I tell him I'll do it.

He pauses, looks at me and asks me if I'm sure. I tell him there is not much to be sure about in ironing a shirt.

146

When he emerges from the bathroom 15 minutes later, he glances at the shirt, then at me, then at the iron.

You haven't kept the iron properly, he says testily. It should be vertical, not horizontal. You'll burn the bedsheet.

That's not true, I mumble. The iron is not even hot anymore.

It was when you switched it off. You should know how to do these things by now, he relents, not kindly, and with the finality of having dropped a fact.

I want to tell him that I know many things, one of which is sticking to a man who keeps a ledger of my failures. But instead, I scrape my thumbnail until it starts to bleed and hurt, after which I push it into my palm, hard. Then I unplug the iron and set it upright.

He picks up the shirt, inspects it from top to bottom, and sighs. It's okay, his voice rattles, which is worse than if it weren't.

I am quiet. S picks up the shirt and smooths it again with the same choreographed care of the first time.

I move to the mirror to fix my face. I like to be in control, but I feel the pressure building behind my teeth. This is also where S realises that he has gone a bit too far, so he comes up behind me and places his hand on my shoulder. My muscles tense at his touch, but I stay still because that's what I do, play along so he continues to be warm.

He then throws me flat on the bed like I was a pair of logs. His weight follows next. His hand reaches for my waist, fumbling the button of my jeans. He paws at my chest before scooping my breast out of my bra. I am repulsed first, scared later.

I lay like that for a few seconds, my body weak with the lack of competence needed to throw him off. I feel ready to disintegrate under S, who had only grown heavier by leeching off me and hollowing me out. A few minutes later, I shove him off with a ridiculous lack of precision, my elbow knocking into his ribs. He stumbles and catches himself against the edge of the bed.

You deserve someone like M, he spits out. *Someone who cheats and still gets away with it. That's your type.*

I am catching my breath, too foggy to have the clarity to process anything. The last time he had said the exact thing, I had begged him to never say it again.

You lean into me without mercy. You take and take and take.

You think that you are better than me. You think I do not see that? But you're just like your brother. Unstable. Disappointing.

I look at him, pummelled by what has been said to me. Then I walk to the iron stand, pick up the iron and hurl it at the television. In an alternative dimension, where only regrets bloomed on the horizon, I would hunt him down. I would rehearse this moment and watch it unfold exactly as it does now. And then, I would end it differently.

***

The next morning, I wake up to nine missed calls from S and a voice message saying he had spoken to the executive editor—a friend of his boss—of the publishing house I'd been reaching out to about my poetry collection. They'd like to schedule a meeting with me.

You're going to be a published writer, baby, he says, his voice thick with glee.

***

Long before S and I got married, I had crashed into an i20, three-and-a-half LIITs down and too floppy to understand the laws of physics or consequence. I woke up barely, to the side of a heart monitor doing its thing, beeping like death in motion, when he said my name.

He pressed my hand and laid his head on my lap, his tears soaking through the hospital sheet for 40 minutes straight. We spent the next seven months admiring the broken and unbroken parts of each other's bodies.

I had decided this would be the man I will not live without. That's what it was like with S—being throttled by the full force of love because he studied it obsessively and did not know anything outside of it.

It was lovely.

It was cruel.

Not destroying what you love is the highest act of love, S says, every time I cannot take us anymore.

We take turns missing each other now.

—ANSHIKA RAVI (she/her)

She brings cold air and a flurry of dead leaves into the lobby. The gush of heat feels good at first, but it will soon feel oppressive and stale. She will sleep in shorts and with her window open, just a crack, invisible from the street below. She has no fire escape, a perk.

It isn't late, but already dark. Her steps quicken as the elevator door ahead starts to close. It's an old building, and to wait again for the singular car is to wait twenty minutes. Her shoes clack along the tile floor like a heavy rain. She needn't rush; a hand untethered from the rest of a body juts out just in time, ushering her inside.

Hairy fingers, nails not long enough to suggest neglect but long enough to have collected black lines of flotsam from the city. She clocks the Help button, and her potential options. She is aware of the small space, the intimate proximity to a stranger, the fact he remained standing toward the middle, not adjusting his spatial footprint to accommodate a second occupant. She makes herself smaller to scooch by him. She stands tucked against the far corner, facing the ancient door as it closes.

"Thanks for holding," she says. The light above an accusation, not in keeping with the wood paneling and dark green floor of the pre-war building.

Taller than her, heavier too. Older, though not by much. Bulky sweater, loose jeans. No coat despite the chill. Receding sandy hair, giving way to grays. Smooth skin that looks more like a child than the middle-aged man he is. Glasses, the kind that remind her of both Superman and Wanted posters. Is he handsome? Is he ugly? Does it matter?

"Sure thing," he replies.

Where do you sleep at night?

"I'm sorry?"

"I asked which floor you're on?"

"Oh, eight. Thanks."

"I'm on nine. Right on top of you."

Headphones in, music off. She thinks of the keys in her pocket, fingers them like a rosary. She thinks of her best friend, tracking her location from her house across the country. They know each other's coordinates, and she is tracking her, too. But they are both at home, so what good does it do?

The elevator groans and slowly ascends. She senses him looking at her out of the corner of his eye. She is careful to look straight ahead at the buttons smudged with other people's fingerprints. She smells the greasy odor of other people's takeout orders, the cold smoke from the cigarette he must have just had outside, and beneath all that, the dank stench of her own sweat forming beneath her coat. The prickle of awareness that could, in an instant, turn to fear. What is the difference, anyway, between awareness and fear?

The cab driver who tried to push his way into her last apartment, the reason she ultimately moved. His spit trailed against the glass once she got the door shut. A moment of uncomfortable, heightened, angry eye contact. She looked out of her darkened window from floors above for an hour, until he left, and slept with plates stacked in front of her door and a knife beneath her pillow.

The men who call her *baby* on the sidewalk, then *bitch* when she crosses the street.

The ones who follow too closely behind her, who like her body when they think it's available, find it revolting as soon as they learn it's not.

Nice tits.

"What?"

"Nice weather we're having," he says.

"Oh. Yeah."

"I was being sarcastic. I'm sick of this cold." Did his voice just get icy? Suddenly, she is aware she is not playing the game right. She smiles brightly and says, I am sick of the cold, too.

The elevator crawls.

Her mother making her change into sweatpants instead of her nightgown when her uncle stayed on the couch. The burn of shame as if this was something important that she should have already known. The early introduction to the lifelong monitoring of men, to ensure they were ok. Uncomfortable at best, tempted at worst.

The grown men who craned their necks out of their cars when driving by as soon as she hit the age of twelve. The friends of her father, fathers of her friends.

Her seventh-grade history teacher said she was mature and pretty for her age. Different than the other girls in class. She blushed. She saw him years later as a high school junior, and he said she'd *really grown*. He blushed. She hated that it felt like power.

The boyfriends who wanted her until they didn't, then wanted her again once they were married. Morphing her into a scab to women she'll never meet. She held a phone full of secrets. The fact that they know she'll never detonate the bombs they've wrapped in candy colored paper and given to her willingly, with a pack of matches.

When her mentor put his hand on her thigh under the table at a work dinner, squeezing it harder the more she pulled away. A smile plastered to her face for the others at the table. He never responded to her emails again.

"I've seen you around the building," he says now, as the elevator groans and lifts. *I've noticed you when you haven't been looking, when you haven't been careful, when you haven't been on your game.*

The silence is thick. She knows there is something she should say, but can't bring herself to.

"Not very neighborly, are ya?"

"Just tired. I'm sorry," she says and hates herself.

Maybe he's lonely, maybe she's cruel. Maybe neither. Maybe both.

Fool me once. Fool me twice, shame on me, shame on me, shame on me.

The elevator opens.

"Have a nice night. See ya around." *I'll be watching.*

She turns left and waits for the suction sound of the door closing, holds her breath. She goes right. Where she lives, where she will forget.

Until tomorrow.

—ALEXANDRA SAVILLE (she/her)

The jelly felt cold against my belly, just as I'd been warned—a wet goo, rubbed eagerly across the squirming bulge that sat tenderly between my hips.

With the pizazz of a magician, the technician brandished the ultrasound wand, spinning slow circles against my sticky skin.

A rapid thumping burst from the monitor, a rhythmic applause.

"A strong heartbeat!" she pronounced. "Everything looks good, Mrs. Chaney. Are you ready to see your daughter?"

Henry gripped my shoulder, his excitement palpable as the technician turned the screen. And then, there she was: thrashing legs, fluttering arms, a bulbous head. 20 weeks, 2 days.

Henry's lip quivered, his eyes brimming with tears. "She's beautiful," he whispered. "Just like her mother."

My eyes remained glued to the screen, startled by a sudden flash as my daughter flapped her hands.

"Are those . . . claws?"

"Hm?" Unaroused, the technician squinted at the monitor. With a flick of her wrist, the wand descended deeper into my womb. Irritated, my daughter let out a swift kick. The technician laughed as I yelped, focusing the splotchy image on her tiny fingers.

"Oh yes!" she exclaimed. "And healthy ones. You know, we often don't see them curve like that for another few weeks. Have you been eating a lot of kale and eggs, Mrs. Chaney? That's the keratin, at its best."

"And her snout?" Henry prompted.

With a jolt, the wand danced across my abdomen. Sure enough, a generous mount could be seen, rotating back and forth as my daughter rocked.

"Well into the 60th percentile. And if you look just over here—" she gestured to a white streak "—you can see her nose. Look at that tip! Pointed up!"

Henry beamed, but I found myself fixated on the screen, in search of any potential abnormality.

"Her ears," I pressed. "How are her ears?"

"Looking sharp. Erect at a 45-degree angle. We'll do a hearing test postpartum, of course. But no doubt she could hear even a branch cracking, up to six miles away."

"And her legs?"

"All the better to chase you with. No doubt she'll be able to take on any non-lycanthrope that crosses her path."

I considered the wolfish figure before me, kicking her paws in amniotic bliss.

"And . . . she will—she will revert back? She'll change?"

The technician nodded solemnly, expecting this question. "Yes, every full moon," she said. "You know, Mrs. Chaney, this is a good thing. She's built tough. Girls ought to be tough in a world like ours. They ought to defend themselves. I can't imagine what it would be like for them if they were built like us. This transformation, it's a gift, evolution at its finest, right before our very eyes."

Her expression grew dreamy. "You know, the body adapts to its surroundings. Sometimes I wonder, if it wasn't for the new regime, if our daughters would still be born the old-fashioned way. The way our sons, poor dears, are still born. They say the first case was almost 20 years ago, the day the first edict was signed. A little girl, born in Maine. Her condition didn't come up on the ultrasound, you know. She transformed at birth, in the delivery room. Imagine the shock!"

Henry laughed, but I was silent, thinking of terror that must have overpowered her mother, the sense of guilt, helplessness.

"They studied the mother," the technician continued. "Sure enough, the lycanthropy had been dormant in utero. And then when she was born, it kicked into gear. A reflex to the world. It activates much sooner these days, at conception."

This wasn't news to me. Henry and I had read the latest studies when we discussed family planning. But the whole thing seemed implausible at the time, like a fairy tale. New realities often do.

"They're still researching the cause. There's a lot of medical debate," the technician mused. "Was it something in the food chain? A reaction to pesticides, growth hormones, climate change? But between you and I, Mrs. Chaney, I think it's modern Darwinism—how would we expect our girls to survive, otherwise? A girl needs a little firepower every now and again."

I cried when I learned we were having a girl. I thought of my own childhood, long before women ran with wolves. I yearned for my daughter to have the same whimsy, those milestones that seem frivolous in hindsight. For summer days making wishes on dandelions, and evenings spent catching fireflies. For Sundays curled on the sofa, nose in a book, dreaming of fantastical worlds. For school plays and science fairs, for graduations and college tours. I'd even settle for a fraternity party or two.

"But she will," I whispered, "be human?"

"As human as you and I."

My voice grew even quieter. "And she'll be . . . pretty?"

"Every full moon," the technician assured me. "For about three days, until it wanes. I've heard it's quite empowering when they embrace their mortal body. It can be overwhelming, that sense of freedom."

I frowned, pondering this.

"And you know," the technician added. "It's not forever. The lycanthropy ceases around proper childbearing age."

That, perhaps, scared me most, but I kept my thoughts to myself.

Henry placed a hand on the back of my shoulder. "She's beautiful, Astrid," he breathed. "Our strong, beautiful girl."

"Our beautiful girl," I repeated, unable to quell the sob that escaped my lips.

—MARIA PIANELLI BLAIR (she/her)

No mother should have to bury her child, but it will be fine, I tell myself. I make arrangements. I have her cremated, and right now I'm pouring her ashes into a plot of soil. They pepper the darker dirt with flecks of grey, falling into a recession I'd made sometime before to make room for the seed, the tree which would save my daughter. I knead her ashes into the dirt with my knuckles as if I'm spreading dough. I wonder how much of her could really be contained in those little crumbs, those grains of her remains, like some forlorn beach in a black and white film. Tears fall into the soil and ashes, forming darkened sunbursts on the surface of the crater. I chuckle at the thought that I was getting a head-start on watering it. I nestle the seed into the mixture and cover it, struck by the memory of tucking her into bed, trying to remember the last time.

***

Ruby is four and I'm picking her up from preschool. The front desk clerk buzzes me in, and I power-walk to her classroom. It's more or less free play when I arrive, part of the end-of-day routine, but Ruby shies in the corner and doesn't come to me.

"It's normal," her teacher assures me, "At least she enjoys her time at school enough to not want to leave!"

"Ruby, now, mommy has to go," I say, putting just a little bass in my voice. I don't want to embarrass her in front of her friends.

"When mommy picks you up, baby, you come to mommy, okay?" I say to her in the car. She nods in the affirmative and stares transfixed out the window on the drive home, pointing out cars and clouds in her little child's dreamland.

***

"Hello mother, it's me, Ruby," the little sapling says.

"Ruby, baby, is it really you?" I say.

"Yes, mother. It's been a long journey."

"Tell me everything, honey."

"They told me this will be difficult for you to hear, but when it happened, my soul left my body. It went down, mother. Oh, don't look so worried. All

157

young souls go there. It's wondrous. An underwater forest at the bottom of the sea, all the branches jutting upward, swaying in the current of the vents beneath them. A robed figure wandered the forest with a lantern lit by the glow of lost souls, its light a pale shade of blue. I felt my soul being pulled toward him. He gave me choices. My memory is foggy after that, but I ended up here."

I collapse to the floor and wake up sometime later.

"Did you have a good nap, mother?" sapling Ruby says.

***

I water her every day. I learn that I cannot leave her in my bedroom overnight or she will talk and talk and talk, as plants never sleep.

"Do you remember the funeral?" I ask her one morning.

"Of course not, mother, that's when I was away, at the underwater place."

***

The day of Ruby's funeral. All I can think as I frown through the gauntlet of bereaved family members is that her coffin looks so small. Somehow its size didn't strike me when I picked it out at the funeral home. I look down at her little face, so serene, so pale against the velvet pillow. My Ruby. I imagine the destroyed flesh and bone at her waist, now covered by a frilled dress I'd picked out just for the occasion. There is a slightly troubled look on her face, as if the muscles contorted with pain as she passed and the agony somehow remained. I think about hunting down the man who hit us that day but know it won't bring her back. Still, a revenge fantasy is one way to pass the time.

I see a man in the corner. A man I haven't seen in some time. Not since I was still pregnant with Ruby.

"Why here, why now, after all this time?" I say to him.

"I came to see her, and to see you. To make sure you're okay," he says.

"Look at me. Do I seem okay? But now that I think about it, it's not unlike you to show up when it's too late. Where were you when I was raising her on my own?" I look over to see the other funeral-goers staring, but I don't care.

158

"Please. I didn't do this," he says.

"Are you saying she'd still be alive if she wasn't with me?"

"I'm not . . . It's just . . . I'm just glad you're still here."

"Don't. Not here. I don't need to be reminded of another past failure."

We leave together. He spends the night. It's the only thing I can do to mourn her without falling apart completely. He wakes before I do and leaves before dawn, his residual warmth still lingering on the bedclothes when I reach for him.

***

After her birth, after sixteen hours in labor, I bring Ruby home from the hospital alone. She cries little, so at least she isn't colic. The phone doesn't ring. Time elongates. She is milk-fed until my left breast stops producing, then I feed her with formula. I rock her and sing to her.

Good night, Ruby

I'll tuck you in bed

Good night, Ruby

Sweet dreams in your head

On and on I sing to her, changing the words a little every time. She notices. I see it in her face, pudgy and round.

***

"Tell me a story, mother?" Ruby asks me just before bed. It's the first time she's asked for one since she came back, but before it was our bedtime ritual.

"Okay. There was once a very sad queen."

"Ooh, I've never heard this one before, goodie. Why was she sad?"

"She lost something very dear to her. She knew that the king was going to replace her the next morning with someone far more youthful and beautiful than she, so she scooped up their daughter, the princess, who was still just a baby, and stole off into the night. There were dangers in the lands surrounding the castle, but the queen chanced upon a wanderer who chose to help them. He fought back great beasts that sought to

159

destroy the queen and the princess, but they were unsuccessful. They made their way to a rival kingdom, where she expressed her woes to the rulers there. They listened to her with sympathy, for her husband the king had a nasty reputation. Attacking would mean outright war, so they devised a plan. The woman who was to be crowned queen had a twin sister who was easily bribed. They swapped her out just before the ceremony, and she slayed the corrupt king before his followers. The people fell into turmoil and reduced the kingdom to ashes, but the queen was free to raise her daughter in relative peace, protected by the rival kingdom and her new companion, who put aside his wandering ways and stayed with her and the princess. She forgot her queenhood and lived a simple life in the village."

"Well, that's not a very good story to tell right before bed," Ruby says. I kiss one of her leaves.

"I'll see you in the morning," I tell her.

***

I begin to have second thoughts.

"Ruby, this is starting to feel unnatural."

"Mother, don't you see that it's right this way? This way, you won't outlive me."

"Ruby, please…" I trail off. Anymore, I can only talk to her for a few moments at a time.

***

"Are you going to give dad another chance?" Ruby asks me one morning.

"That man is not your dad. He's not even your father. He never was, so don't grace him with that title."

"There must have been something that drew you to him in the first place," Ruby says. I huff over to her pot and lift her up, sticking her in the closet.

"Mother, no, please," Ruby pleads, but I pretend not to hear her. I close the closet door, her muffled voice leaking through as I walk away.

***

160

"Actually, the real reason I came here was to tell you about something. It's an ancient practice I picked up from one of the refugees at work. You don't have to lose her," Ruby's father says to me as we lay in bed, the night of the funeral. "They say it's a way of redirecting a soul, in this case, into a tree. All you have to do is put her ashes in with the soil." He leans over and fishes something out of his pants pocket. He produces a seed, wrapped in a crinkled manila envelope, a strange red symbol stamped on one of the corners. It looks old and weathered, as if it's traveled many miles and traded many hands to get here.

"This is the seed you must use," he says, placing it in my hand and closing my fingers over it, sealing it, willing it. The ritual begins.

***

"Mother, did you go to the underwater place like I did?"

"No, Ruby, I went somewhere else, where older souls go. It was... darker than the place you described, like a poorly lit library. I had to find my way by feel, trying to read some pattern in the letters I felt inscribed on the shelves. It seemed like I wandered for a long time, but my eyes never adjusted to the dark."

"You didn't have eyes then, mother."

"And I don't have them now."

"It's okay, we don't need them. This is enough."

"It is. Agreed."

***

Ruby's father visits us from time to time, bringing us gifts and sitting there on the grass for a while. Sometimes he cries, other times he laughs. Once, he got furious and stormed off. I wonder what he was thinking about then. What is he thinking about now, as we speak not to him, and he not to us. We just sit in silence together, feeling the breeze. And yes, he does come up and hug us on occasion. We don't really mind.

***

The roads are icy. I'm dropping Ruby off at elementary school. If only she gets out on the other side. If only she doesn't have to run behind the car

161

to get to the sidewalk. Whiplash is all I get out of the ordeal; all else is taken from me that day.

When the ambulance pulls away, I can't bear to ride along. I can't see her like that. The look on the paramedic's face as he closed the doors isn't exactly reassuring. His eyes are averted, downcast, falling bombs.

***

I put it in my will that my ashes be buried along with another special seed some distance away from Ruby. The first few months are maddening, as my voice is not yet loud enough to reach her, but over time, I grow large and our conversations stretch on for months, then years, then decades, as the landscape changes and time marches on with its glacial persistence.

Every so often, when the wind allows it, we can actually touch branches. I can feel a cold front coming in. Perhaps we can muster the courage to reveal ourselves to passersby and convince one of them to tie our branches together. I feel just a little bit warmer when our leaves are touching, almost as if we're holding hands.

"Good night, mother."

"Good night, Ruby."

—G.W. McClary (he/him)

NONFICTION

"You're gonna feel a pinch and then pressure on three, okay?"

I laid on my back lifelessly. I'd heard what the doctor said over the blood rushing and pounding in my ears, but I couldn't summon the strength for a response. She slid her head out from behind my leg to make sure I was still awake. Loss of consciousness was one of the symptoms she rambled off pre-procedure like a prescription medication infomercial where all the people are smiling while doing everyday tasks in slow-motion. Seeing me stare blankly at the drop-tile ceiling, she swiveled her chair back into position, hiding again beneath the exam sheet spread between my legs. I tried to lose myself counting the dots like stars on the foam, ceiling squares above me. I made it up to around a dozen before I winced at the sharp sting.

"You've got it, Mama", the sweet, southern nurse said as she squeezed my hand and rubbed the inside of my forearm.

The doctor slapped a gloved hand on her thigh and sat fully up to give the nurse a dirty look above her glasses. She tsked and gave a slow head shake before descending between the stirrups once more. Without uttering a word, we both got the message loud and clear.

How could you possibly call her Mama when she's just lost her baby?

Though I knew in my heart it was a harmless, even endearing sobriquet, I understood why the doctor was upset. If I were one of the countless women she'd assist in that same room desperately trying to hold onto motherhood, that small four-lettered word would land like a bullet. But on that same exam table, I laid there only desperate to make it through the next half hour.

Just then, I felt a blunt, heavy pain somewhere deep inside me I didn't know existed. I curled my toes and felt my knees begin to shake violently in revolt. I looked to the nurse for comfort and found it immediately. She sympathetically looked down at me with a familiar concern all mothers have when their children aren't well, and mouthed silently once more, while dabbing the sweat and tears rolling from my cheeks, *you've got this.*

—**AMANDA IZZO** (she/her)
Previously published in Ana Magazine

"Watch out for my windows. You're gonna break them. And mind my plants."

My mom shouted at me from the kitchen. I was practicing my football passes and moves in the backyard outside the kitchen. Our lawn was bordered by the chickencoop and bike shed on the one side, and the garden plants on the other. The chickens were my audience and if the ball hit their run, they protested like they were away-team supporters. Lucky for my mom, no windows broke, and no plants were harmed in the process of becoming a better football (soccer for North Americans) player.

"And stop ruining your shoes. The noses are all scuffed."

All my shoes had scuff marks, lovingly restored by my mother on her Friday afternoon shoe polishing session. I found out that you could play football in wooden clogs too, should the need arise or when my mom got too angry about a new pair of shoes being ruined.

At school, all the boys wanted me on their football team during recess football games. Some boys said:

"Wish you were on our Saturday team. As goalie. Or center forward. Ours are rubbish."

I did not know what to say. There was no point. Girls were members of the gymnastics club that trained in the community hall beside the school and went to recorder lessons—which I hated. These were the days before all female football teams and joining the local boys' team for practice and matches would have been out of the question, however good I was. I could not. Not legally.

So I played at school. With the boys. And at home with the chickens.

Growing up, I did not want to be a girl. I wanted to be a boy and be like my dad. Whenever I could, I'd slip into the barn where he was working in the sweet earthy smell of hay and cow dung, leaving my sister with my mother in our farmhouse kitchen. My dad and my Opa were the ones who did the real work, in my eyes.

And men wore pants instead of uncomfortable dresses. I hated my flowery home-made dresses when I played football at school.

Boys had more opportunities and freedom than girls.

The men in our village could choose between the farm or the factory. Boys were stronger, not smarter per se, but could become farmers and drive tractors like my dad whereas girls only became mothers and wives. They stayed home and did not go anywhere besides the Friday morning grocery shopping run.

Although, when I was a teenager, my dad did not mind teaching me how to drive our tractor, like the village boys of my age. Perhaps because he was an all-girls father his perspective on learning that skill changed.

It seemed that dads and granddads did all the cool stuff in my Dutch village: chase cows when they broke free, ride tractors across bumpy fields, bring in the potato harvest in a cloud of black dust, fix tractors while breathing in the heavy scent of black grease, whereas the moms ran the household and made sure our clothes were washed and food was on the table, all while helping out with farm chores such as feeding the young Frisian calves before they were old enough to graze in the fields with their mothers. Our moms did the boring stuff. To an outsider it may seem as if I grew up in a rural idyll.

An idyll for whom?

Would all the women have agreed that being a housewife and a mother was their dream job?

Two women in the village led a different life.

Beside our female teacher Miss Hetty, who taught the first three classes in our red roofed two-classroom school, there was Aart's mother who worked as a nurse in the regional hospital. She was the only working mom at our school. We thought it was weird that Aart's mom worked. Who was there when he came home from school? His dad did not have any cows so perhaps she did not need to help on the farm? His family grew corn, potatoes, and sugar beet. It did not occur to us that perhaps his father made sure he came in from the fields when Aart came home from school, or that his mother worked nights and was there in the afternoons.

These two women were the female role models in our—population 300— village who worked outside the home and off the farm.

Only later did I learn that women often did not have a choice. Society forced them to stay at home. By law or by convention.

I now know how that law affected women. My mother-in-law, as a civil servant, was fired upon marriage. Her entire generation had the start of their married lives dictated by a law that considered being married and working outside the home as morally reprehensible. The horror. What if schoolchildren were confronted by a pregnant teacher! As if children did not come into contact with their own mothers when they were pregnant with their brothers and sisters-to-be.

Until deep into the sixties, and in my village deep into the seventies and early eighties, it was the norm that women stopped working once they were married, even though the Dutch law requiring them to stop working upon marriage was revoked in 1957. Men still saw it as an abomination when women kept on working after they married. Those women who continued in paid employment after 1957 stopped after they gave birth to their first child. That seemed a definitive cut-off point.

My mom told me she had moved across the country in December of 1970, from the seaport city of Rotterdam, where she worked in a care home, to our farm in the sticks near the Dutch-German border to marry my dad. Here, she was expected to run the household, help on the farm, and take care of us kids once we arrived. As I would within a year. Village society, and her live-in in-laws, would have frowned upon her searching for a new job. Once married you did not work. Not outside the home or off the farm. Not in the sticks.

How lonely.

And what a waste of skill and talent.

Now the days of laws—and of society—deciding whether a woman can be *someone* else besides a wife and mother are gone. In my case, I was the first woman in my family to go to university in the early nineties. Although the battle over women's destinies and bodies is far from over. I can't begin to list the examples from across the globe.

How can the female body still be a battleground?

And I wonder if the modern-day 'trad wife' knows what hard-won battles their foremothers fought to be able to continue working after marriage. So there was a choice.

Do they know how unhappy these mothers had been after the forced termination of their employment? How dreams and hopes were crushed? How their mental and physical health suffered?

Do they realize how vulnerable one is without paid employment or social status if a relationship breaks down or a partner turns out not to be the fairytale prince? How do you cope financially and psychologically when living the traditional dream lands you in divorce and destitution?

With high divorce rates in Western countries—50% of American marriages fail—women have to do their own saving. Adhering only to traditional gender roles could land them in dire straits.

For centuries on farms, however, the working situation has been different; there, wives have always worked alongside their husbands. Farming requires a team effort.

Combining work and motherhood is not easy but mothers have been doing just that in agricultural societies since the dawn of time.

But being raised on a farm, I felt women only did boring household chores that were on a repeat cycle every day, like a washing machine that would not stop. The rhythm of a woman's day revolved around breakfast, lunch, and dinner. And around washing, drying, and folding. And around mending clothes and dusting off children who had—once again—fallen and came running to them for comfort and band aids. And not to forget cleaning, again and again, when sand and muck appeared on floors as it always does on farms. What is outside tends to come inside like persistent dung flies.

Later, I realized that women were the glue on and off the farm. Without them, the whole ecosystem on the farm and in the village would come grinding to a halt. Without food cooked, no labor. Without a well-kempt home, what was there to come home to after a day in the fields, and how could a man work without clean and mended clothes?

But that did not change the fact I hated girls' play such as playing with dolls. The area of play for *proper* girls that mimicked the taking care of babies and the household tasks assigned to women.

I did not care for dolls and babies; I played with tiny metal cars in the sand box, and I liked climbing trees, building huts in the treelined verge in front of our house, and I loved playing football in the backyard with my mom shouting to mind her plants and windows.

Besides football practice at home with my sister, I played on the dirt football field at school. In a mixed team with the boys. Boys who were members of the village football team and got to play on our local team's grass football pitch that lay just behind the school. I could only dream about playing on that field, dream about playing for the village team. My goals or saves were only applauded by my classmates. How well—or not—I played was invisible for the rest of the world, like the work my mother and the other farm wives did.

At school during recess, I wanted to split myself in two: I wanted to be the center forward scoring goals and be the goalie stopping the balls from hitting the net. I could not trust anyone it seemed to either score goals or keep my team from being defeated while watching the ball hitting the net behind the goalkeeper. Our designated goalie just stood there watching the ball fly past. Again, again, and again.

I resigned myself to being the goalkeeper. That was the only way to make sure my team did not lose. It might not result in us scoring points, but we would not get any missed saves either. I took one for the team and stood in the goal.

And I played. I played. And I played. Every day.

Until I left primary school at twelve.

At secondary school we did not play at recess. That wasn't cool anymore. My football practice days were over. We only played during gym classes occasionally.

In 1986, when I was at secondary school for two years, the Dutch football federation introduced mixed teams for the under twelves. It was too late for me, but this at least meant that girls did not have to travel far to play football in an all-girls team but could join a team in their own village or neighborhood, like my classmates had wanted me to.

But things are slow to change in my province. For the 2026/2027 season the professional football team in my corner of the province, Football Club Emmen, will start a girls team for the first time in its history.

That is almost forty years too late for me. And now I can't play football games anymore since the aftereffects of pelvic girdle pain in two pregnancies put a stop to my running days. For the last two months of both my pregnancies I walked with crutches. Now I can do almost everything, but playing football matches would be too big of a risk.

I am not the first person in my family to give up playing football at a certain age. In his day, my dad had been a quick center forward. But in my youth, he only sprinted across the fields to catch a cow that was about to break free. He was short and stocky like my Humpty Dumpty grandmother, but unlike her he could run like the wind chasing storm clouds across our fields. He gave up football when his ankles gave out, but in our cow-studded fields he was the center forward.

We all have to make sacrifices for our long-term health.

As I had.

But how does one go from center forward, goalie tomboy to becoming a mother?

It actually comes quite naturally. You can be a kick-ass working mom shadowboxing and playing football with your sons while cooking meals, cleaning, and doing the endless cycle of washing while working outside the home. Someone who says:

"Oh, you just go right ahead and climb that tree."

"Sure, I'm fine with you jumping from the top of the climbing frame."

"Come on, let's play football!"

And that doesn't mean you only have to wear yoga pants, leggings, or sweatshirts. I fell in love with the once hated dresses and other "nice" clothes again. I embraced that side of being a woman.

Center forward and/or goalie, farmer and/or housewife—women can be anything they set their sights on. They can take up different roles at different stages of their lives. Let no one tell you otherwise.

Stay in the game. Swing back that leg and play ball.

Kick the ball in the net. Hard.

Move the goalposts when you have to. For all our sakes, men and women. We all have skin in the game.

—SARA STEGEN (she/her)

Our rivalry began when I was in my mother's womb, suspended in amniotic fluid. It was fated, I now know, because there is always a favorite, even if the words are never spoken. Even if they are. The favorite, however, isn't a constant, meaning that being the favorite for a period of time doesn't protect you from becoming quietly loathed. Despite the best efforts of both parents to not replicate the favoritism that permeated their own upbringings, it is a given. There will always be favorites.

My mother used to tell me I was her miracle. She had desperately wanted to give my sister a playmate. After several miscarriages, she became pregnant with me at 35-years-old and was heavily monitored throughout gestation to ensure she wouldn't lose me. I was born healthy, although I didn't speak until I was three, and even afterwards, I had to go through intensive speech therapy until I was eight.

"Maybe that's why you turned out so *smart*," she'd say to me in front of my sister as we got older. "Because you're *special*." My father once told me that I had *brains* while my sister had *beauty*.

Why can't you be more like—? It was said to her as often as it was said to me, except at different life stages.

When I was a toddler, my sister teased me with our shared toys, many of which were originally hers. One morning, she came close to me in the hallway, waving an Aladdin doll in front of my face as I backed away.

"He's going to get you!" she shouted, centimeters from me. I lost my balance at the top of our staircase and fell backwards. One-by-one, I rolled down each carpeted stair, my mother screaming when she found my contorted body writhing in pain on the first floor. While there were no lasting injuries, the act sowed a divide between us that lasted throughout our childhood and beyond.

***

"Why is it that you turned out so lazy?" my father said, peering at my sister from above his newspaper. I was standing on my tiptoes and washing the dishes, the hot water filtering through my fingers as though I were submerged in a jacuzzi. Our house was freezing, and we rarely turned on the heater, so the warmth was a treat. I had commented on how much fun I was having, watching the food be gobbled up by the garbage disposal, the shredded chicken disappearing into the ether. I knew she hated doing chores, so I had eagerly volunteered to show my parents that I was a better daughter than her.

I beamed as my pre-teen sibling looked at the ceiling, twirling a long piece of dark hair away from her tube top. "Don't roll your eyes at me. Have some respect," my father spat through gritted teeth, his fists clenching. My stomach turned as it always did when he raised his voice. I never knew what was coming next, so I dried my hands and scurried up the stairs before I vomited out of fear.

It was around that time I regularly found my toothbrush knocked onto the floor from my bathroom counter, the colorful bristles placed perfectly facedown as if by magic. I told my parents, aware that if my sister was the culprit, she would be punished. My father walked up the stairs, his boots thumping against the wooden floors, and called my sister into the bathroom.

"That's your sister's toothbrush?" my father said, gesturing towards the travertine tiles. "Well, here's yours." Her toothbrush was tossed into our cat's litter box. My sister wailed as my mother ran down the stairs to boil water, explaining that it would be as good as new once it was cleaned. "I *hate* you," she said, staring at me in disgust.

It didn't help that we were nothing alike. Where she was rebellious, loud, and strong, I was acquiescent, quiet, and weak, often crying when I felt threatened. My mother described me as sensitive because I spent much of my childhood on the verge of tears. From ages five through eight, I cried nearly every day at school. Until I was 12, my parents hesitated dining out since I would cry whenever we sat down to eat at restaurants.

"You're going to cry," my sister would say, knowing that she would push me over the brink. "I can tell."

I'd hold up the menu to cover my face and swallow hard. "No," I'd respond. "I'm fine."

"Stop it," my mother would interject. "You're going to make her cry."

"Don't lie," she'd continue. I'd stare at a light fixture or mark on the ceiling, the tears welling up before I had a chance to stop them. "Well, it's just that . . ." I'd choke, my nose scrunched up and red.

"Don't be such a baby," she'd smirk, glancing in my father's direction for his approval. Despite his harshness to both of us, he favored me because I was obedient and did well in school. He called me his "little buddy" and took me on errands, even the ones where he introduced me to beautiful women who were his clients, colleagues, or friends. My sister and I were in a competition for our father's love, and we both were playing to win.

I often hear that a child's first bullies are their parents, but I wonder if siblings have ever been accounted for. When I went through puberty at an early age and gained weight, my father commented on my eating habits, resulting in my withholding of food. When my sister's body also changed, the comments were transitioned to her. I silently observed the cruelty, relieved when it was directed at someone other than me.

My parents divorced after I graduated from high school, and I became the rebellious one. My sister stayed behind to live with my father, while I moved two hours north of our hometown with my mother, marring the increasingly uncertain relationship I had with my dad. My lifestyle, which had been especially studious up until that point, became one that involved college parties and heavy drinking. I gained fifteen pounds, and my sister was sure to detail the exploits she saw unfold on my social media to my parents.

"Why don't you give all of your clothes to your sister?" my mother said, assessing my frame. I overheard her speaking to my sister about my apparent downfall, especially as I navigated mental health issues for the first time.

When I infrequently had lunch with my father during my freshman year of college, he'd recount everything my sister had told him about my college life, focusing heavily on my alleged promiscuity.

"I'm depressed," I explained, "I'm seeing a therapist." We sat in a McDonald's that marked the halfway meeting point between us. I twirled a French fry in a pool of ketchup, miming that I was eating but hoping to take the remainder of the meal home so I didn't have to eat in front of him.

"You're not depressed. You're normal," he responded, "You had a great upbringing. You have no reason to be depressed or act this way." He stared at my soggy fry, pausing momentarily. "By the way, is it true that you've been meeting up with guys from the Internet?"

My sister was everything I was not to my parents: the beautiful one who had her life together save a challenging relationship with her long-term partner. I was the problem child, even though my decisions were directly correlated to the hurt I was experiencing after learning of my father's innumerable affairs. She told me in passing that her boyfriend thought I was a *whore*, and I called her a snitch and wondered why she was so hell-bent on sabotaging my relationship with my family. I desired the closeness with my father that had briefly been there, but I decided to let it go.

When my sister and her partner eventually separated during my early twenties, I chose to be there for her during her most vulnerable moments. My sister and I spent more time together than ever before, and I realized that we had been unfairly pitted against one another from the start. The qualities that had been so different should never have been compared in the first place. It was our mutual though distinct yearning to be accepted by our parents, and although we never acknowledged it, I knew we were both sorry.

***

"You know, you've always been my favorite," my father spoke into the microphone during his speech at my sister's wedding, several years later. My best friend, who was in attendance, turned to me with a shocked expression. I no longer hated my sister. I wasn't envious. I considered where my resentment truly resided in that moment as I stared at the sad silhouette on stage, the man I had been so desperate to please—*He looks terrible*, my mother mouthed to me. I nodded my head in agreement.

—T. HARRISON (she/her)

The streets of Gamcheon Culture Village in Busan were narrow and teeming with tourists. Ice cream shops, K-pop merch stores, and Instagram photo ops lined the block, making it far more touristy than even Gyeongbokgung Palace in Seoul, which I had visited just before coming to Busan. It was my first time in Korea, so naturally, I was hitting all the most famous attractions.

The entire village was on a steep hill, and I was glad I chose to wear comfortable walking shoes. My boyfriend, Sathya, and I weaved our way out of the crowd up a flight of stone stairs, admiring the colorful houses around us—green, blue, pink, yellow. There was a small museum with free entry that explained the history of the village, from its origins in the 1920s to the post-Korean War era, when it became populated by a fringe religious group. The village and its residents were relatively poor until the early 2000s, when the city government decided to revitalize the area by bringing in artists to paint murals, build sculptures, and add some much-needed color to the area. It became an attractive destination to visit, hence the crowded streets Sathya and I were navigating.

"There's supposed to be a market around here somewhere," I said, looking at a map.

"I think we need to go back down the hill," Sathya said.

Given my horrible sense of direction, I simply nodded in agreement and followed him. We were no longer near the crowds, and the street we were on was much quieter and more residential. Most of the tourists were probably still in line to take a picture next to the *Little Prince* statue, which seemed to be the most popular of the Instagram photo ops.

After wandering through the winding roads for another few minutes, we finally spotted the sign for the market. Since it was still early in the morning, the market was empty, except for an old lady selling *gochugaru*—Korean red pepper powder, a key ingredient in kimchi.

I don't remember the first time I ever ate kimchi, in the same way I don't remember the first time I ever drank water. It's always been a part of my life. Whenever I would get sick as a child, Mom would make *kimchi jjigae* for me. Sometimes we would even put kimchi on pizza. Our fridge always had a big jar of kimchi in it, and when I left for college, Mom made sure I had some in my dorm's mini fridge too. It only made sense for me to buy some *gochugaru* straight from the motherland. Sathya looked around the rest of the market while I attempted to communicate with the *ajumma*.

"*Anyeonghasayeo*," I greeted her shyly.

"*Anyeong*," she said back with a smile.

I looked at the massive bags of the red pepper powder, the spicy scent filling my nose. The smell always reminded me of Mom.

"How much for this?" I asked, pointing to a medium-sized bag of *gochugaru*. I thought about how I used to watch my mom make kimchi and how long it would take her to salt the cabbage, leaving it to sit in big blue bins, then blending up the *gochugaru*, garlic, ginger, sugar, and fish sauce to make the paste. It was a labor-intensive process, but I wanted to try making it on my own instead of just buying the jars of kimchi from H-Mart. I figured this *gochugaru*—the good stuff from Korea—would finally motivate me to make kimchi from scratch.

The *ajumma* selling the gochugaru weighed the bag.

"Where you from?" she asked.

"America," I said. "I live in New York City. It's my first time in Korea. I—uhh, *umma hanguk*." I didn't know enough Korean to put a whole sentence together, so I had to settle for "Mom Korean" and hope she understood. I showed her the lockscreen on my phone—a photo of me with Mom and my younger siblings.

"Ahhh, you family?" she asked. "You mom Korean?"

"Yes," I said, "but she lives in America."

"You need more," she said, looking at the medium-sized bag I chose. "This not enough for you mom." She went to get a bigger bag. I knew it was probably a sales tactic, but she was right. I was planning to give some of the *gochugaru* to Mom and my siblings when I got back to the States, and with the bag I had chosen originally, there probably wasn't enough to share between the four of us.

"This one better," the *ajumma* said, plopping a massive bag on the scale. It was about three times the size of the one I picked out, and I would definitely be able to give everyone in my family a good amount of *gochugaru*.

"Much better," I agreed. "Thank you!"

***

A couple months after the Korea trip, I decided it was finally time to attempt making kimchi by myself. I picked up two huge heads of napa cabbage at the grocery store and bought a container online that was specifically for storing kimchi. In my tiny Manhattan kitchen, I rolled up my sleeves and washed the cabbage, ready to get started. I followed a recipe I found on TikTok, watching the woman in the video demonstrate every step of the process.

After salting the cabbage, leaving it to sit, and blending the kimchi paste with the *gochugaru* from Busan, I put on a pair of disposable gloves, grabbed a fistful of the kimchi paste, and started coating the cabbage leaves in it. I loved how tactile the process was, feeling the cabbage and the paste between my fingers—cold, crisp, and squishy all at once.

I thought about the *ajumma* who sold me the *gochugaru*. It was evening in New York, which meant it was morning in Korea. I imagined she was opening up her *gochugaru* store for the day, scooping heaps of the scarlet powder into plastic bags for customers. I thought about Mom and my childhood, hoping the kimchi I was making would turn out half as good as hers.

"Ooh, it's starting to smell like kimchi in here," Sathya said.

"Try some!" I popped a bit of the fresh kimchi into his mouth.

"Whoa, it's so good!"

I loved living with a partner who was excited about my heritage and interested in my cultural foods. I wished Mom had had the same. I suppose one could say that my father, a white man from New Hampshire, was somewhat interested in Asian culture, but only in the sense that he was interested in Asian women. Once, when I was a child, I found a porn DVD in my dad's closet. The cover had two naked Asian women on it. I was only nine or ten years old, and though I didn't fully understand what I was looking at, I knew it was something I wasn't supposed to have seen.

If my dad and I were out somewhere without Mom, he loved to tell Asian waitresses and cashiers that he had an Asian wife.

179

"Your English is really good!" he would tell them. "Where are you from? My wife was born in Seoul."

As much as my dad liked to talk about Mom's heritage, I don't recall him ever really taking the time to learn about it. When I would watch BTS music videos, he would joke about how he thought all K-pop boy band members looked like girls. One evening, he had a friend from work over at our house for dinner, and Mom had a jar of kimchi fermenting on the kitchen counter. His friend made some comment about how, when he was in Korea for work, he tried kimchi and hated it.

"I just couldn't get past the smell," he said. "I couldn't believe people there ate that every day!" My dad laughed, and I wondered if Mom, who was sitting at the table with them, was hurt that her husband hadn't said anything.

After I finished college and moved across the country, my father had an affair with a Filipino woman, which eventually led to my parents' divorce. A few years later, he married a woman from China.

The last time I saw him was before his wedding, which I did not attend. Not that he sent me an invitation. He had a work event in Boston, where I was living at the time, and asked if he could see me. I invited him over to my apartment for dinner. I made *samgyeopsal*, rice, spinach, and bean sprouts. It was a meal that Mom had made for him hundreds of times over the course of their nearly twenty-five year marriage.

"What's this?" he asked me, picking up a piece of pork belly with his fork.

"*Samgyeopsal*," I said in disbelief. "You've had it before. Mom used to make it all the time. Don't you remember?"

"Oh, no, I don't remember that."

"Do you want some kimchi?" I asked. "I just got a new jar of it from H-Mart."

"No thanks," he said, making a face. "I never liked it that much."

Mom spent so much time making kimchi—making all the food—for our family. It was as though my father hadn't noticed any of it. Or at least hadn't appreciated it. Food was how Mom connected to her Korean heritage. It was how she showed us she loved us. And my father couldn't be bothered to care about any of it.

I knew how lucky I was to have Sathya. We cooked dinner together almost every night. He loved Korean food, and always supported me as I explored my relationship with Korean culture. And of course, I loved when he would make Indian dishes that his mother used to make him when he was a child, like dosas and rasam. We both understood that food was the thread that kept us tied to our heritage.

***

Several weeks after I made my first batch of kimchi, I decided to make *kimchi jjigae* with it. I had gone through most of the container already, and the kimchi that was left at the bottom was beginning to sour—perfect for *kimchi jjigae*. Sathya cut up a block of tofu while I scooped a dollop of gochujang into a pot.

I dropped the last of my first batch of kimchi into the pot, listening to it sizzle. I added a spoonful of the *gochugaru* from Busan for extra spice. We dumped the rest of the ingredients in the pot and let it simmer. Onions, sesame oil, spam, minced garlic. The salty, spicy aroma filled our apartment.

It smelled like home.

—**MADISON BLOCK** (she/her)

ABOUT THE CONTRIBUTORS

✳ **Abigail Kirby Conklin** (she/her/hers) is an educator and writer currently based in Toronto, Ontario. She is the author of the 2020 chapbook *Triage* (Duck Lake Books), the forthcoming chapbook *Self-Animal Inventory* (Red Ogre Review), and a variety of other works that can be found in the *Tule Review, Sugar House Review, Elevation Review, Lampeter Review,* and *Wild Roof Journal.* She's online at abigailkirbyconklin.us and @akc_poetry_prints

✳ **Agneya Singh** is a writer and filmmaker from India whose work explores themes of resistance, memory, ecological collapse, and political grief. His debut feature film M Cream received multiple international awards, and his recent poetry engages with lived experiences of war, occupation, and environmental devastation. Based between India and Malta, he is currently completing a novel set in Kashmir.

✳ **Alexandra Saville** is a writer and communications professional based in Brooklyn, NY. Her essays have appeared in *Business Insider, The Other Cape, SheWrites,* and others. Her fiction has appeared in *The Marlowe Review* and *The Dumbo Press.* www.alexandrasaville.com

✳ **Alexis Raymond** is a poet that writes to honor the minority experience in predominantly white spaces. A Stonecoast MFA graduate and an Ashley Bryan Fellow. She is also a journalist, and published short-story fiction writer. Her work can be found in *Portland Monthly Magazine, The Elevation Review, So to Speak Journal, Moonstone Arts' Fatal Force Anthology,* and *Hellbender Magazine.*

✳ **Amanda Izzo** (she/her) is a writer and artist from Boston, MA. Though published in other mediums, she has enjoyed the art of creative writing for over a decade. This year, she has begun to share comprehensive and detailed recollections of her life and youth in the form of nonfiction narratives. Her newest pieces titled, "Tell Me Where it Hurts" and "Consent Defined" were published by *Levitate Magazine* in May 2025.

✳ **Ana Dee** (she/her) is a confessional poet and the author of *Untouched* (2023). Endlessly curious and drawn to the beauty in darkness, her poems explore themes of intimacy, longing, and identity. Ana is the winner of the 2025 Central Avenue Publishing Poetry Prize and her words have found homes with *Button Poetry and Sunday Mornings at the River.* She believes every poem is a secret: some whispered, some screamed. Find her on Instagram @anadeewrites

✳ **Annastacia Stegall** (she/her) is a poet and MFA graduate from Eastern Washington University. She currently serves as a lecturer at Gonzaga University, teaching English Composition. Her work has appeared in publications such as *Peatsmoke, #Ranger, Gordon Square Review, Bifrost,* and *Expressions.* Annastacia resides in the Inland Northwest with her feisty cat, Roscoe. Find her on Instagram at anna_stegall.

✳ **Anshika Ravi** (she/her) writes short fiction and essays. She is currently a writing coach at an MNC. She aspires to write women the world loves to hate. She is always, constantly dreaming of a freer, safer life outside her home country, India. Her fiction has been published in *The Hooghly Review.* Her non-fiction has been published in *The Indian Express, Outlook, Firstpost, Mint Lounge, FII,* etc. She can be found at @anshika_ugh (X) and @catpersonetc (IG).

* **Aref Malemi** is an Iranian poet, born in 1996. His published works include *Pause of the Storm* and *Individual Gathering*. He has received several awards, including recognition at the Wingless Dreamer International Festival in India, as well as national honors such as the Mim Moayed Festival, the Simorgh Festival, and the Faraspid Festival.

* **Arya Vishin** (he/him) is a mixed Kashmiri-American & Jewish writer from the Bay Area. He is a PhD student in Comparative Literature at Harvard.

* **Azalea Aguilar** is an emerging Chicana poet from South Texas, where the scent of the gulf and memories of childhood linger in her work. Her poetry delves into the complexities of motherhood, echoes of childhood trauma, and the resilience found in spaces shaped by addiction and survival. Her work has appeared in *The Angel City Review*, *The Skinny Poetry Journal* and *The Acentos Review*. She has been the featured poet at events hosted by The American Poetry Museum in DC.

* **Brooke Harries** (she/her) is from California. Her work has appeared in *Annulet, Denver Quarterly, Laurel Review, Puerto del Sol, North American Review, Salamander, Sixth Finch,* and elsewhere. She has an MFA from UC Irvine and a PhD from the University of Southern Mississippi. Currently, she teaches English at Rocky Mountain College in Billings, Montana.

* **Carla Schick** (they/them) is a queer, nonbinary activist writer who sees poetry as creating alternative narratives. Their works have appeared in *Fourteen Hills, Forum Literary Magazine, Qu* and *Black Fox Literary Magazine*. Their work has also been anthologized in *Colossus: Body and Currents*, *Querencia Press* and *Pure Slush*. They are the recipient of a 2023 Nomadic Press/SF Foundation poetry prize. They hold a Certificate in Creative Writing/Poetry from Berkeley City College.

* **Catherine Shonack** (she/her) is a Brooklyn-based writer from Torrance, California who obtained her master's degree in playwriting and dramaturgy at the University of Glasgow. Her poetry chapbook, *breakup notes from a love story i made up in my head*, was published by *Bottlecap Press* (July 2025). Her poems have been published in *Ink Sweat & Tears* and *Abundance Literary Magazine*. She has had various plays performed at several different scratch nights in London, Glasgow, and Leeds.

* **Cecilia Savala** (she/her) is a Shrek-obsessed Latinx poet, teacher, and mom who writes about gender, body image, generational trauma, and cultural detachment 1200 miles from home. She is a morning person, a cat person, a creative writing teacher at ASU, and the Virginia G. Piper Fellow-in-Residence. Her work can be found in *Acentos Review, The Boiler,* and *Poetry South*, among others. Follow Cecilia at @cecsav on Instagram.

* **Celia Lan** (she/they) is a bilingual writer from China exploring hybrid forms of expression for life writing across genres. Their work often meditates on memory, diaspora, and queer identity, seeking language as both refuge and experiment. They consider poetry a passage into the unknown and are currently preparing for a Creative Writing PhD.

* **Chanice Cruz** (she/her) is originally from Brooklyn, NY, however, credits Richmond, VA, for introducing her to the slam poetry world. She is currently an Open Mic coordinator at Kew & Willow Books in Queens, NY and is a co-host for The Poet & The Reader Podcast. Her poems have been published in Newtown Literary, Sinister Review, and several other literary magazines. She received her bachelor's degree from Queens College. Now lives in New Rochelle with her fiancé and two cats.

✳ **Cypher**, (she/her) is a self-taught brown and queer Tamizh diaspora poet living in Canada. Her work has been featured by the *Dark Winter Literary Magazine, Ontario Poetry Society, Arcana Poetry Press, the Ophelia Gazette,* an several others. Cypher is currently working on her first full-length poetry collection - *The Self is an Ocean* - which is slated for release in July 2026. You can find Cypher on Instagram: sruthi_amalan_0.

✳ **Davi Schweizer** (they/them), from Philadelphia, is the hottest poet you know. They are the author of *Only Seconds Until Detonation* (forthcoming, Querencia Press) and *Echo Decay* (Kith Books). Their poems have appeared in *JAKE, BULLSHIT LIT, Line+Stars,* and other places. They are the editor and founder of *Troublemaker Firestarter.* Follow me on Twitter: @trblmkrfrstrtr, Instagram: @troublemakerfirestarter

✳ **Devon Webb** (she/her) is an autistic writer & editor based in Aotearoa New Zealand. Her award-winning work—spanning poetry, prose, reviews & personal essays—has been published extensively worldwide & accumulated seven Best of the Net/Pushcart nominations. She is currently working on her debut novel & full-length collection among other creative pursuits & can be found on social media at @devonwebbnz.

✳ **Dion Farquhar** has poems in *New Words Press, Non-Binary Review, Superpresent, BlazeVOX,* etc. Finishing Line Press published her third poetry book, *Don't Bother,* last fall. She works as an exploited adjunct, still loves her students, and is active in the University of California Santa Cruz lecturers' union, UC-AFT. Website: https://dionfarquharpoetry.cargo.site/

✳ **Dixie/Damon Kootz-Eades** (It/its pronouns for now) lives in Kansas City with its polycule, puppy, and cats. It is currently working on its MA in Literature at the University of Central Missouri, and after that has set its eyes on writing a queer, literary fiction novel.

✳ **Edward Daschle** (he/him) is a queer writer living in Maryland. He has attended Clarion Workshop and Disquiet Workshop, and earned his MFA in creative writing from the University of Maryland, where he now teaches. His stories appear in *Apex Magazine's Robotic Ambitions anthology, After Dinner Conversation - "Best of 2023" anthology,* and *Washington Writers' Publishing House,* among other venues.

✳ **Elena Lucia Perez** is a Mexican-American storyteller who divides her time between writing, film, and theatre. She earned her BA in writing from UC Riverside and is editor-in-chief of *The Metaworker Literary Magazine.* She lives in Los Angeles where she works as a film editor and spends her free time curled up with a good book, craft-making, or photographing nature. Other things she likes are: fruits, outer space, dragons, and puns. Find her on Instagram and Bluesky @ELP_storyteller

✳ **Eliza Fixler** is a therapist, animal lover, and nature enthusiast living in Pittsburgh, PA. Some of her previous writing is published in *GASHER, Chaotic Merge,* and *mutiny! Magazine You can follow her writing at @elizafixlerpoetry.bsky.social.*

✳ **Eva Lynch-Comer** (she/her) is a Pushcart Prize–nominated poet with an MFA in Creative Writing from Hollins University. She is the author of the chapbook *Sonder* and has been published in over 20 literary magazines. Eva is an African American and Afro-Latina poet with Costa Rican ancestry. In her free time, she enjoys singing, drinking tea, and reading graphic novels. You can find more of her work at www.evalynchcomer.com and on Instagram @evalynch321.

✳ **G. W. McClary** (he/him) is a native of Ohio with a B.A. in literature and founder of The Storycraft Co-op. His stories have appeared in *Nova Literary-Arts Magazine, The Haunted Portal, Razzle Dazzle Cafe*, and elsewhere.

✳ **Jaime Rodríguez** (he/him) is a Chicano poet from the Rio Grande Valley. His work blends English and Spanish to explore queer desire, cultural silence, and the natural world of the borderlands.

✳ **Jenny McBride's** writing has appeared in *The California Quarterly, DASH Literary Journal, Common Ground Review, Streetwise, Grub Street Literary Magazine*, and elsewhere. She makes her home in the rainforest of southeast Alaska.

✳ **Jessica Bates** writes poetry, fiction, and creative nonfiction, and lately her work explores the paradoxes of parenting. Jessica lives with her partner & two kids in Tennessee. Find her obsessively reading, watching spiders build webs, or scribbling poems on old receipts.

✳ **Jorie Logan** (she/her) is a published poet & professional copywriter originally from Virginia's Appalachia & now residing in Transylvania, Romania. Her work blends lyrical romanticism with reflections on spirituality, nature, the human condition, surrealism, philosophy & more. She passionately weaves authenticity & raw emotion into her work. Beyond writing, Jorie is an old soul with a young heart who enjoys traveling, community volunteering, leading a book club, & facilitating a spiritual circle.

✳ **Joylyn Chai's** writing has appeared in *The Fiddlehead, The Ex-Puritan, Ricepaper, The Cincinnati Review,* and elsewhere. Her essays have been nominated for a Pushcart Prize and selected as notable for The Best American Essays 2024. Joylyn is Chinese-Jamaican Canadian and teaches adult learners and newcomers on the traditional territories of Tkaronto/Toronto.

✳ **Kath Healing** (they/them) is a queer, trans, disabled, and neurodivergent poet from the UK, now living on the unceded lands of the Ləkʷəŋən-speaking peoples (Victoria, BC). Their work explores myth, memory, and survival, often blending ecological imagery with queer embodiment. Winner of the 2025 Victoria Writers' Society Poetry Contest, their poems appear or are forthcoming in *PRISM International, CV2, Plenitude* and elsewhere..

✳ **Kieran Fu** is a queer, wasian, and neurodivergent poet currently rooted in Chicago. Their work centers on love, loss, family, and belonging. You can find some of their work in the *Passionfruit Review, Oyster River Pages,* and on Instagram @kierxpoems.

✳ **Lorena Maria** (they/them) is a Latine poet and writer presently living in Central New Hampshire. When not writing or reading, they enjoy spending time by the ocean, exploring used bookstores, and visiting friends in far off places. You can find them at @lmdotcom on instagram.

✳ **Louis Aletando** lives and works in Sacramento, California. He is an educator with a special research interest in the mystical traditions of the Middle Ages.

✳ **Madison Block** (she/her) has a BA in journalism from the University of New Mexico. In 2018, she won the Albuquerque Authors Festival nonfiction writing contest. Her work has appeared in *Korean American Story, Burnt Pine Magazine, Mom Egg Review,* and *The Nasiona.* Madison currently lives in New York City and works as a marketing manager at a nonprofit.

✳ **Mae Fraser** (they/she/he) is a hopeless romantic poet from the New Hampshire seacoast. Their work has been published with *Sheepshead Review, Cool Beans Lit,* and *Northern New*

England Review, among others. She has work forthcoming with _Juste Milieu Zine, Argyle Literary Magazine,_ and _Rat's Ass Review._ They received a BA in English - Creative Writing from Salem State University. You can find them online @maeflowerreads or under their gigantic pile of unread books.

✳ **Maria Pianelli Blair** (she/her) is a writer and multidisciplinary artist. Her fiction has been published in _Gypsophila Magazine; swim press; two-headed press; Pile Press; Prosetrics Literary Magazine;_ and _StepAway Magazine._ Her artwork has been published in _Contemporary Collage Magazine; FEELS Zine; Photo Trouvee Magazine;_ and _45th Parallel,_ among other publications, and nominated for the _Best of the Net_ anthology. You can follow her on Instagram @strange_sunsets.

✳ **Maxwell Bauman M.F.A.** (he/him) is Owner/Editor-In-Chief of _Door Is A Jar Literary Magazine,_ a print and digital publication now celebrating its 10th year. He is a contributor to _Chicken Soup for the Soul._ Maxwell is the Lead Editor of _Aggadah Try It,_ an imprint of _Madness Heart Press._ He is the author of Jewish horror short story collection _The Revised Anarchist's Kosher Cookbook_ and the novella sci-fi/ fantasy _The Giant Robots of Babel._

✳ **maya cordero** is the founder of _DISCOUNT GUILLOTINE._ she loves love and she hates the united states.

✳ **Nicholas Olah** (he/him) has self-published four poetry collections, _Where Light Separates from Dark, Which Way is North, Seasons,_ and _You Are Here._ Olah's work appears or is forthcoming in _Humana Obscura, Thimble Literary Magazine, Wildscape Literary Journal, Door Is A Jar Literary Magazine,_ and more. Olah's poem, "On the Drive Home", won third place in The Poetry Lighthouse Prize in spring 2025. Check out more of his work on Instagram at @nick.olah.poetry.

✳ **Nico Ricciardi** (he/they) is a transgender writer and college student currently residing in Arizona. His work has appeared in _Penumbra: Literary and Art Journal_ as well as the _WILDsound Writing Festival._ When he's not writing, he is usually at the public library, thinking about writing.

✳ **Phaedra Saffron** (they/them) is a writer and violist from Greece, currently based in the Netherlands. Through their poetry, they experiment with visual forms and rhythm, pushing the boundaries of their artistic ideals. They attained BA and MA in Classical Music at HKU Conservatory, a MA in Arts curated by the Global Leaders Institute, and studied writing in the International Writers Collective. Currently working on a novel, a fabulist, hypermodern, neuroqueer experiment on fantasy writing.

✳ **Pulkita Anand** is an avid reader of poetry. Author of two children's e-books, her recent eco-poetry collection is 'we were not born to be erased'. Various publications include: _Tint Journal, Origami Press, New Verse News, Green Verse: An anthology of poems for our planet_ (Saraband Publication), _Ecological Citizen, Origami Press, Asiatic, Inanna Publication, Bronze Bird Books, SAGE Magazine, The Sunlight Press_ and elsewhere.

✳ **Samn Stockwell** (she/her) has published extensively. Her new book _Musical Figures_ is published by Thirty West Publishing House. Previous books won the National Poetry Series and the Editor's Prize at _Elixir._ Recent poems are in _Pleiades_ and others.

✳ **Sara Stegen** is a Dutch poet and non-fiction author who writes about land, family, nature, and neurodivergence. Home is a boulder-clay ridge in the northern Netherlands where her bike shed contains 8 bicycles and where she is working on a memoir about apples and autism and her first poetry collection.

✳ **Sarah Daly** (she/hers) is an American writer whose fiction, poetry, and drama have appeared in fifty-five literary journals including *New Feathers, Moss Puppy Magazine, Shot Glass Journal, The Avalon Literary Review, and Autumn Sky Daily.*

✳ **SJ Larsen** (they/them) is a non-binary Washington-based writer and proud cat mom. They gravitate toward heavy topics with intentional playfulness through tone, shape, and message. Their work appears in *Manastash Literary Magazine, Free Spirit Publishing*, and most recently *Poet's Choice.* They are a recent graduate of the Creative Writing Bachelor's program at Central Washington University.

✳ **T. Harrison** (she/her) is an American writer and photographer. Her artwork and essays have appeared in *Cosmic Daffodil, Yellow Arrow Journal, The Shuffle* and more.

✳ **Tanja Lau** is a Swiss-based poet and writer with German-Italian roots. A highly sensitive observer and mother of two, she explores life's complexity with vulnerability and a hint of humor. She studied Comparative Literature before venturing into entrepreneurship. Her first children's book is scheduled for publication in 2026, and several of her poems are forthcoming in anthologies. Her writing can also be found on Instagram @tanias.butterflies and on Substack at taniasbutterflies.substack.com.

✳ **tommy wyatt blake** is the jester of popular culture and poet laureate of timefuckery. they are the author of many books, including *For Your Entertainment!* (Troublemaker Firestarter, 2026), *Mutually Assured Destruction* (Ethel Zine, 2025), *DITCHLAPSE / [REALLY AFRAID]* (Querencia Press, 2024), *So, Who's Courage?* (Bullshit Lit., 2023), *Trick Mirror or Your Computer Screen* (fifth wheel press, 2022), and others. he is currently synthesizing digital archives, space voids, and confines of the body.

✳ **Tracy Chenxi Shi** (she/her) is a poet, translator, and mixed-media textile artist writing about dislocation, connections, the reachable, and the unreachable. She seeks out things, protracted happenings, and elusive threads linking time, history, and the individual, questioning and seeking how we, as living beings, navigate the complexities embedded in timeless human universalities.

✳ **Valyntina Grenier** is an LGBTQIA multi-genre artist living in Eugene, Oregon. She is the author of three poetry chapbooks and one full length collection. You can find those books at Finishing Line Press, Cathexis Northwest Press and various places where books are sold.

✳ **Vic Brooks** (they/them) is a duplicitous queer gender-shifter writer living in London, and parent to an octopod (small identical twins). Their novel, *Silicone God*, was published by *MOIST Books* (UK) and *House of Vlad* (US). Find their essays, short fiction and poetry in *The Philosopher's Magazine, Wrong Directions, Midcult, Archer, t'ART, W0rms, SAND, Discount Guillotine*, and elsewhere. They are on Instagram @vics_double_trouble.

✳ **William Brasse** is a thing of shreds and patches. Born and raised in Tennessee where his best friends were trees and drugs. Exiled to California where his best mind was destroyed in the hungry maw of traffic. Having nothing to lose, he writes. Novels, stories, plays, essays. Always looking for a way out that never appears.

9 781963 943498